The Rose Canyon Gang

Rose Canyon was far more forbidding and desolate than its name implied. A rugged notch carved into the face of Arizona's Yavapai Mountains, it sheltered few living creatures in its depths, other than for Dane Hollister and his small band of men, all recently fired without reason from their jobs on the MM ranch.

Dane didn't like the feel of any of it. The MM owner, Madison McGraw lay in his bed dying slowly. His foreman the brutish Frank Baker had taken what seemed a series of high-handed actions, including their firing. Some of Dane's crew were ready to give it up and ride out to new country. Dane was just about to forget the matter himself when young Roberta Madison was driven from her own land by Bruno and his men. Then the Rose Canyon gang – men and women alike – knew that it was time to head into battle.

The Rose Canyon Gang

Owen G. Irons

A Black Horse Western

ROBERT HALE · LONDON

© Owen G. Irons 2012
First published in Great Britain 2012

ISBN 978-0-7090-9276-6

Robert Hale Limited
Clerkenwell House
Clerkenwell Green
London EC1R 0HT

www.halebooks.com

Typeset by
Derek Doyle & Associates, Shaw Heath
Printed and bound in Great Britain by
CPI Antony Rowe, Chippenham and Eastbourne

ONE

On the eastern slope of the rugged Yavapai mountains the long canyon carved into their bulk wound its way from the high country to spread out as it reached the grasslands below. Rose Canyon, as it was called, was no different from a hundred other notches in the gray hills except that there was a flowing spring at its head. The water did not run long above ground, but trickled away and vanished after a short half-mile. At the site of the spring the man who had first explored the canyon discovered a wild purple rose growing. How it had gotten there, or where the plant was now was anyone's guess.

Rose Canyon sheltered only yucca, patches of nopal cactus, mesquite and a few scattered and broken sycamore trees.

All in all it was not a hospitable place – too deeply cut into the surrounding landscape for any breeze to reach; hot and dry and isolated, it seemed to shun mankind. Except that now it sheltered a handful of men who preferred its forbidding aspect to being gunned down out on the desert.

'I guess we're up against it for sure now,' Toby Leland

said. There was an unhappy sincerity in the young cowboy's words, as if finality had touched his perceptions.

'We are, and so what?' Sparky – Bill Sparks said, looking up from the small campfire the four men sat circled around. The low flames danced and splashed alternate light and shadow over their faces. Sparky was the youngest of them all, but he was brash, able to deal with their situation more easily than Leland. Or that was the impression he gave, the image Sparky strove for. Red-headed. freckled, he was wiry in build, his hands and muscles always moving not quite in coordination, as if he had somewhere urgent to go but did not know where.

But then, none of them did.

Until recently all had been employed by the Madison-McGraw ranch. The MM brand was the outfit they rode for. Now they were drifters in the wild.

'I can understand you not being as upset as Leland,' Dane Hollister said. He was older, bulkier; darkly handsome despite a receding hairline. He had been to school somewhere; for he was always reading and had a couple of books in his saddle-bags even now, along with his wire-framed spectacles. 'At least you know why you were fired, Sparky.'

Sparky flared up briefly. 'It was nearly dark!' the redhead said excitedly. 'I'd been branding for ten straight hours.'

'And branded a Double M calf with a double W?'

'It was getting dark and I was dead tired.'

The fourth member of their party, Drew Tango, who was reputed to be a former gunfighter, or possibly a lawman gone bad, spoke up. 'It was more than careless, Sparky. It was dangerous. They could have thought you were doing that on purpose, trying to steal cattle.'

'That's what Baker did accuse me of,' Sparky said, referring to the brutish foreman of the Double M.

'What'd you tell him?' Tango asked, poking at the fire with a stick. 'That it was so dark that you couldn't tell which end of the calf was up?'

'Oh, never mind,' Sparky grumbled, seeing that he was going to get no sympathy from these three.

'It is true,' Dane Hollister said, 'that at least you know why you were fired – even if it was only an excuse. The rest of us have no idea why we were cut loose.'

'At round-up time!' added Toby Leland. 'And where around here are they going to come up with four riders?'

'Must have already had some men on the way,' Tango guessed. He shifted his position slightly and dropped the twig he had been playing with into the fire.

'Do you think so?' Dane Hollister asked thoughtfully. In the glow of the firelight he resembled some stuffy professor quizzing a student with a weak hypothesis. Men had made that mistake, taking Hollister for some sort of bookworm; they had frequently learned a lesson. Dane was a man who didn't mind brawling, and he usually came out on top.

'Yes, I do,' Tango said and the others paid attention, knowing that whatever side of the law he had been on in the past, Tango knew something about these matters. 'Not even a crazy man, or one given to rages as Baker is, would fire half of his crew at round-up time. And the way we were let go – there had to be some planning behind it.'

Hollister nodded agreement. 'Why'd they tell you they were firing you, Leland?'

The young man said irritably, 'Baker told me I missed

7

six cows up in the Carrizo Gorge. Said I probably hadn't even bothered to go up there to look. That's not true! I rode that patch of ground for five hours – there weren't any strays up there.'

'What about you, Dane?' Tango asked.

'Me?' Dane Hollister leaned back, propping himself up on his elbows. 'Baker said that the boss lady – Roberta Madison – claimed that I was annoying her in an ungentle-manly manner.'

'Did she?' That didn't sound like the young woman who was a partner in the Double M.

'I don't know! How could she have said such a thing? I spoke to her seldom, and when I did, I can assure you it was in a respectful manner. I have many faults, I suppose, but I was raised to be a gentleman.'

'Did Baker let you confront her?'

'Of course not. He said something to the effect that it would only disturb Roberta.'

Sparky asked Tango: 'And you, Tango? Why'd they fire you?'

'One of the boys, Gomez, told me it was because Baker thought I was a dangerous man to have around, that I was probably an outlaw anyway.' Tango's eyes briefly drifted away. Sparky had heard stories about Tango, many of them, and he thought that there might have been a kernel of truth in them. But the tall man had made no trouble since he had arrived on the MM last winter.

'Baker said nothing to you?'

'No,' Tango said with a thin smile. 'But when I rode into the home ranch on Tuesday, I found my good saddle and my bedroll on the porch of the bunkhouse. I didn't need an invitation to leave.' Tango shrugged, 'I just figured the hell with it, switched saddles and rode off.'

'So here we are,' Leland said, as miserable as ever. 'What a fix! Any of you have an idea what to do next?'

'Some of the big ranches near Tucson would probably take on a man for the duration of the round-up,' Sparky thought.

'That job wouldn't last long,' Leland said. 'Double M is already putting a trail herd together. Most of the big ranches will be doing the same thing. You'd probably get paid off at the end of the drive, and that would be that.'

'At least I'd eat a while longer,' Sparky answered. 'If you've a better idea, I'll listen.'

'That's the thing – I don't.' It was Toby Leland's first time away from home; and he had no experience with 'dragging the line' – looking for work or handouts until the next opportunity for employment presented itself. Leland had tried to make a life for himself, a man among men, and now figured that he had failed in that endeavor.

'What are you thinking, Professor?' Sparky asked Dane Hollister. For a moment the big man's eyes darkened despite the glow of the fire.

'I told you never to call me that,' Dane replied, speaking softly. There was obvious menace in his voice. Sparky rapidly apologized. There was a reason for Hollister hating that nickname, but whatever it was, he kept it private. Dane shook off his irritation and answered the question:

'It's obvious to me that Baker was looking for a pretext to fire us. His reason for discharging me was absurd, as he could have discovered if he had bothered to ask Roberta Madison. The reasons for firing Leland and Sparky are equally flimsy. Even if both criticisms were true, a man

9

would usually be let off with a warning, not fired out of hand.

'As for Tango here . . . I think that what Gomez told him is the absolute truth – Tango might prove to be a dangerous man to have around.'

Tango started to argue, saw Hollister's point and shut his mouth. 'So you think Baker is up to something? I do too, Dane.'

'What?' Sparky asked. 'Taking the cattle, stealing the land?'

'Those aren't unknown occurrences,' Hollister said. 'I don't know for sure, but he's up to something.'

With the old man, Kent Madison, laid up in bed and McGraw now dead, Roberta virtually held title to the Double M Ranch. And Roberta, unfortunately, had not been raised to manage such a responsibility. Her father had wished her to have an easy life, a happy childhood. While a son might have been urged to learn the cattle business, the art of ranch management, Roberta had been encouraged to buy new dresses down in Dos Picas, to ride her horse early in the mornings, to cultivate the arts, to be a hostess and a future wife. That was the way things were then, certainly the way Kent Madison wished them to be.

'What are you thinking . . . Dane?' Sparky asked, stumbling over his tongue at the last word. He had almost said 'professor' again.

'I'm thinking,' Dane Hollister said, eyeing the other experienced man, Tango, 'that we ought to try to find out why we were really fired. Why the four of us. Not Gomez, Allison, Kramer or Sully.'

'So far as we know,' Tango said.

'So far as we know, but Roberta Madison would have

certainly noticed if her entire crew had been dismissed, and demanded to know the reason why. She might trust Baker to run the ranch as her father did, but firing everyone would have been a little much, even with new men coming in. I think Tango is correct on that point. I have to believe that Baker had already hired men to replace us. And they will be tough men, wouldn't you think, Tango?'

'You'd have to believe so.'

'Then,' Sparky said, 'they just got us out of the way to bring in some men that Baker wanted working there.'

'Maybe. But it must go deeper than that.' Dane Hollister encouraged them: 'Think, boys! What makes us different? Is it something we've seen, something that's a threat to Baker? There must be something behind all of this.'

'Meantime, we don't eat,' Leland complained.

'Oh, we'll eat,' Dane promised. 'Maybe not what you're used to or what you like, but a man with a rifle will only go hungry if he's an idiot.' Dane lowered his voice. The young man was still obviously frightened by his prospects. 'Leland, if you don't want to stick with us, we understand. Same goes for you, Sparky – if you want to try to hook up with one of those big Tucson ranches, that's your decision.'

'What is it you are planning?' Sparky wanted to know, The fire was burning low now. His face was shadowed, deeply concerned. Dane Hollister answered him:

'I'm going to find out what's wrong on the Double M. Kent Madison took me on when I had no place else to go, He was kind and generous to me. When I had . . . when I had nothing, he trusted me. He's old and sick now. I won't abandon him.' Hollister was silent for long minutes. No one else spoke up. At last, staring across the low glow of

11

the dying campfire, Dane Hollister asked:

'What do you think, Tango? Will you ride with me?'

Tango stretched his arms lazily and reached for his blanket. 'I've nothing else to do,' Tango said, then he rolled up in his blanket to fall off to sleep. There were only embers in the fire pit now, low and golden. Above, the silver stars shone across a blue-velvet sky.

'I'll stick,' Toby Leland said from out of the darkness. 'I'm like Tango – I've got no place else to go, nothing else important to do.'

Sparky had his blanket over his face, but his muffled voice reached them. 'If everyone else is willing to gamble, I'm staying too.'

The four men slept long if not well, and when the glare of the white sun found the depths of the canyon it was well into mid-morning. Tango was the first awake and up. He considered starting a fire, but the cold he was feeling was in his bones from the chill of the desert night, not from the dry air in the canyon. Leaving the others he walked to the head of the gorge where the artesian spring bubbled up out of black basalt stone and bathed as well as he could.

On returning to camp he found the other three awake, if sleepy-eyed. 'What do you figure we need to do first?' Tango asked Dane Hollister. Leland spoke up in a some-what childish voice.

'We need to eat first.'

Sparky and Tango both smiled. As they knew, Leland had not yet suffered a man's deprivations. Life in the wilds, on the desert, could lead to days of going without food. Although Leland did not know it, he was a pup among wolves. He considered himself a tough customer now, after having worked on the range for almost four months. Still, he had hardly ever been deprived. The Double M set a good table for its ranch hands.

'I've got some salt biscuits I snatched from Cooky,' Sparky volunteered. 'And, if I'm not mistaken, half a ham somehow found its way into my poke as well.'

'Set it out,' Dane Hollister said encouragingly. 'We'll eat first, then we'd better make sure all of our canteens are full.'

'And then?' Tango asked, crouching down beside the cold fire pit.

'We need to think things through first, Tango. As I asked last night, why were we four the only ones run off the ranch?'

'We already discussed that,' Toby Leland said, accepting two biscuits from Sparky who was slicing the ham he had laid out on a square of oilskin.

'Discussed it and come to the conclusion that all of the reasons given us were sham ones,' Dane said. He nodded his thanks as Sparky served him two salt biscuits and a wedge of ham. The sun was bright in Dane's eyes as it peered over the upper reaches of the canyon. He shielded his vision with one hand as he fed himself with the other. 'Where's my hat?' he demanded after some moments. Sparky sailed it to him. Dane tugged the brim low and continued:

'Where have we been, what might we have seen – together?' Dane asked.

'You still think that Baker's up to something crooked?' Sparky asked.

'I think that Frank Baker has been up to something since he shed his swaddling clothes,' Dane replied sourly. He drank from his canteen to wash down the dry biscuit and ham.

'There was one time. . . .' Sparky began, but then he shook his head, declining to continue.

'Come on, Sparky. If you've got any kind of notion, spit it out,' Dane encouraged the redhead.

Sparky stood there, chewing on his own roughly made sandwich; the persistent probing of Dane Hollister's eyes prompted him to continue.

'Do you all recall,' Sparky asked, 'the day that the summer storm with all the close thunder and lightning scattered the beeves up along the north pasture and they took to the forest up along Mammoth Point before they tired themselves out running and lost themselves among the pines?'

'I remember,' Toby Leland said. 'Do you have another slice of ham to spare?'

'I recall it, too,' Tango said. 'There was just the four of us up there to circle around through the woods and drive the steers back on to their graze.'

'That was the day . . .' Dane Hollister now looked as thoughtful as any professor, 'the day we came upon Baker and those two citified gents talking along the ridge. Remember, Tango, two town men riding in a buggy?'

'I recall. Baker asked what we were doing out that far and we told him. But he didn't say a word about what he was doing up along the Mammoth with those two strangers.'

'No, and he didn't look all that happy about seeing us there,' Sparky remembered. 'He tried to smile, but it was like a buffalo trying to smile. He was angry inside.'

'He was seething,' Dane agreed. 'But why? What could he have been up to?'

'I don't know,' Tango said, 'but it's too strong a coinci-

14

dence for me, seeing that we were the four hands cut loose. And it's about the only time I can ever remember us riding together.'

'That was only because of the stampede,' Dane remembered. 'We were the only hands available around the bunkhouse that day. As a rule, none of us partnered up. Certainly not the four of us.'

Dane Hollister fell into a studied gloom as the others finished their scant meal. Tango rose and saddled his lean sorrel pony. The animal was not a cutting horse, although it performed well enough. The long-legged, gleaming animal with the white blaze on its nose was a running horse, the sort that only rich men and outlaws could afford. Rich men for their pride, outlaws as a matter of necessity when outrunning the men with the badges. Tango took pride in his pony: but men were reluctant to ask how he had come by such a horse.

After tightening the double cinches on his Texas-rigged saddle, Tango returned to stand near Dane Hollister who was still deep in thought. Tango stood with one leg slightly hooked, his well-worn holster with its blue Colt .44 riding low on his hip. Sparky watched the secretive man with a sort of admiration, Toby Leland with something approaching envy. Wherever Tango went, men would know that he was a force to be reckoned with. Never loud, never the sort to strut, a man knew with just a casual glance that no good could come of having Tango for an enemy.

'What do you say, then, Dane?' Tango asked.

The serious-minded Hollister lifted his eyes. 'I believe that there are at least three things we have to do. First, we have to find a way to talk to Kent Madison.'

'The man is dying, they say. No one's going to let us go

up to see him.'

'Dying or not – and we don't know if he is – the Double M is Kent Madison's ranch. He should be the one making decisions, Perhaps he doesn't even know that Baker has fired us all.'

'I don't see how we can get in to see him. Even one of us,' Leland said.

'Through Roberta,' Sparky said with a grin that offended Hollister. It seemed to imply that Dane's only interest was with Roberta Madison.

Dane did not respond, although his eyes grew a little colder. 'Second, we have to try to find out who those two strangers were. Someone in Dos Picos must know – the stage line, the hotel manager, They didn't just appear from nowhere for no reason.'

'I can take care of that,' Tango suggested.

'I'll go with you,' Sparky offered.

'I don't know if that's a good idea. If there's trouble at the ranch, we don't want Dane to be by himself.'

'I can ride with Dane,' Leland said, apparently feeling that he was being overlooked and slighted by the implication that he could not provide adequate protection for Dane Hollister.

'We'll keep an eye on the Double M,' Dane said. 'Baker is bound to ride out on to the range sooner or later. That will be the time to try seeing Kent Madison.'

'You said you'd come up with three things we should try,' Sparky recalled.

'Yes,' Dane said with a sigh in response to the red-headed kid's words. 'The third is closely connected with the first. I need to talk to Roberta. If her father is in as bad shape as they say, the ranch will fall to her, and she needs

16

to know that something that might affect her legacy is going on on the Double M.'

Dane looked around as if expecting someone to smirk, smile or make another remark about him and Roberta, but he was met with three poker faces.

So what if he did love the girl! That had nothing to do with matters. Or did it? In truth, would he have hung around, hiding out in Rose Canyon, if he had no liking for her? Maybe not, but he did have an obligation to Kent Madison as well. Dane banished his equivocal thoughts and rose, strapping on his own well-worn Colt revolver.

'Will you ask Roberta a question for me?' Tango asked. 'Ask her how her father's partner happened to die. What is the truth behind Calvin McGraw's death? People don't talk about it much, and when I met McGraw he was in his early fifties, and seemed healthy.'

'As healthy as Kent Madison did not so very long ago,' Dane responded.

'Just that healthy,' Tango said then he turned on his heel and walked to his sorrel. He gathered up its reins. 'Well, are you coming or not, Sparky! It's a long ride to Dos Picos.'

TWO

'How have you got this planned, Tango?' Sparky asked as they approached the dusty, low-built town of Dos Picos. Beyond the desert settlement the two peaks from which it had gotten its name rose: gray, desolate and barren.

'I intend to have a cup or two of good coffee and a decent breakfast – nothing against your effort at thinking ahead with the ham and biscuits, but the thought of eggs or a steak has been haunting me for the last ten miles.'

'That's not what I meant,' Sparky said as his dun horse mis-stepped and jolted him in the saddle.

'I know it,' Tango said with a tight smile. 'I was just trying to figure it out myself. Dane would know – he's a fig-uring sort of man. I guess we do as he suggested; we ask about two strangers arriving on a recent stage, two men checking into the hotel the night before the summer storm. Maybe the bank, the telegraph office. I guess there's a lot of possibilities.'

'The saloons,' Sparky offered brightly.

'That's up to you,' Tango said with a distasteful grimace.

'I guess you don't drink; is that it, Tango?'

'I guess I don't,' the tall man answered, sparing only the briefest of glances at the young red-headed man.

'What was it you did before, Tango? I mean, I always hesitated to ask you. Back there. But, I'm kind of the snoopy sort, if you haven't noticed. This is just between the two of us. It can't be spread around the bunkhouse now. What brought you out here? Who did you use to be?'

A quarter of a mile passed beneath the hoofs of their horses. Sparky was certain that he had stepped across the line, invaded Tango's privacy and was expecting no answer, when Tango said:

'I suppose it doesn't matter any more. As to who I used to be, that goes back a long way and covers a lot of territory. My last job,' the tall man said without looking toward Tango, but rather into his past, 'was as a security guard with the railroad. I rode the rails looking for troublemakers, or, if we had been tipped off that there might be an attempted robbery, it was my job to halt it. I did that for two years altogether.'

'Why did you quit?' Sparky asked with real interest 'Sounds like an interesting life.'

'It was interesting,' Tango agreed. 'And I did my share to make certain that the railroad was safer to ride than it had once been.' He paused.

'And then?' Sparky asked, pursuing the point. They were near enough to Dos Picos to see sunlight reflecting off the glass of the windowpanes facing the southern sky.

'I shot the wrong man,' Tango said without inflection. 'I was drunk. Too quick to draw; too slow to think. They fired me.'

Sparky tried to absorb the information. It seemed all too credible and explained a lot about Tango. 'Does that mean you are a wanted man now!' Sparky asked.

'Not for that,' Tango dissembled. 'The railroad bought the man's family off. It turned out he had a shady past anyway, but he wasn't out to rob anybody on that day. As for the rest,' Tango shrugged, obviously having had enough of talking about himself, 'I haven't ever seen any posters out on me. I could be wanted here and there – I wouldn't know; I make it a rule not to revisit places I have been before.'

They entered the town limits of Dos Picos. The shadows slanted long across the rutted main street of the desert town. Tango had one more comment.

'Kent Madison knew about this and a lot of other things I'll never admit to you, yet he offered me a job, refuge when I was at the end of my rope, unable to think of a way out except to go bad. He trusted me. Don't ask me again about my past, Sparky, and don't ask me why, when I swore allegiance to Kent Madison and the Double M brand, I meant it.'

They stabled their horses at a shabby-appearing establishment called Tonio's according to the weathered sign hanging on its adobe-block front wall. The interior was hot, smelling of dung and straw; poorly maintained, it seemed. Yet Tonio's was probably one of the most thriving businesses in Dos Picos. After all, besides the occasional stagecoach there was no other way to travel. Even men who arrived without a horse would soon find themselves in need of one. For the rest of the town – well, it looked like it had been weather-whipped and sun-beaten for centuries although, so far as Tango could remember, there had not been a single person dwelling there other than a few Yavapai Indians up until twenty years ago when a brief, disappointing silver strike had occurred there. The people who had remained behind after the silver had played out seemed to be mostly tired old men and women too weary of life to travel on and start over somewhere else.

It was the sort of town where a dog fight on Main Street was considered entertainment. Mostly old men sat in the shade and dreamed of days past and the young hoped for a future. All were disappointed. This was Dos Picos, after all, where dreams did not long survive in the withering glare of the desert sun.

There was a lot of drinking – all-night drinking, all-day drinking. Whiskey prodded a few more dreams into temporary reality. When the whiskey faded, the dreams faded and men seemed to shoot each other out of sheer frustration.

Tango knew a lot about towns like this, too much about the influence of alcohol, which was why he had declined to join Bill Sparks in a trip to a local saloon, even knowing that Sparky was correct: there were a lot of loose lips, a lot of information to be gathered in these places where men had little else to do but gossip.

Tango went first to the only hotel in town, a wooden two-story building painted a gaudy shade of orange with dark green color splashed across the front door and on the window frames. The woman behind the desk was bulky, flabby and smothered with too much powder. She smiled as Tango entered from the hot, sunny street, then let her smile sag as she realized that he was only there for information.

'I do remember them,' she answered in response to his question, 'They came in on the afternoon stage – what was it, month ago? The night the thunderstorm hit.'

21

'That would be the day.'

'One of them looked like a walrus, if you know what I mean. The other was scrawny and nervous – wore a pencil-thin mustache.'

'That describes them pretty well,' Tango said. 'What did they do while they were here?'

'Outside of hiring a buggy from Tonio, I wouldn't know,' the hotel clerk replied thoughtfully. 'They were here and then they were gone. Paid promptly and caught the next coach east.'

'Well, I thank you,' Tango said, sliding one of his last remaining silver dollars across the counter. The woman's sad eyes brightened a little.

'Sorry I can't tell you any more about them. You ought to ask at the bank.'

'The bank?' Tango asked with surprise. 'Why there?'

'Didn't I mention that? They had some kind of meeting with Amos Blount. They were over to the bank for a couple of hours. You should talk to Mr Blount.'

After getting directions to the bank Tango crossed the street diagonally as a heavy unloaded freight wagon rolled past. He noticed that the town marshal's office was directly in front of him. He became instinctively wary. He still did not know if what he had told Sparky was correct. There may have been Wanted posters out on him that he was unaware of. That was something he hadn't worried about for a long time. Out on the range, working on the Double M, he had a safe haven. It didn't matter if someone was looking for him, he could never have been found on that isolated ranch. In town, even a tiny, withered town like Dos Picos, there was always the chance that he might find someone carrying a paper with his name printed on it.

No one stood at the door of the marshal's office, no man with a star watched from the windows. The bank was of adobe block as well, painted or whitewashed to a pale, summer-blistered ivory hue. There were iron bars on the front windows, no windows at all to be seen on the side of the bank that faced a dusty, littered alley. The wind was rising now; a stray dust-devil made its swirling way down the street, picking up leaves and paper in its passing.

The sign on the bank said 'open' and Tango swung the heavy oaken door open and went on in to the somewhat cooler interior of the lobby. A man with bleary eyes, wearing a too-tight black suit stood behind the single teller's cage. There was a neatly lettered sign reading 'Mr Preston' hanging over his head.

Preston looked up at Tango as he entered, with that mingled look of concern and hope common to small-town bankers. They never knew when a slick-dressed man might be a bank robber or a scruffy old man in near-rags had maybe just struck a mother-lode of gold in some lonesome canyon.

'May I help you?' Preston asked with practiced formality.

'I want to talk to Amos Blount.'

'Concerning. . . ?' Preston asked, studying the tall lean man with the dust of the desert on his clothing and the slick Colt .44 revolver on his hip.

'It's a private matter,' Tango said, leaning his forearms on the counter as he smiled at the cashier. He knew what Preston was thinking. Had he been the cashier, Tango would have had the same doubts.

'I'll see if Mr Blount is available,' Preston said, making a point of theatrically locking the cash drawer with a key that he wore on his gold watch chain.

An unsmiling Tango waited until the cashier reappeared, followed closely by a florid, round man with a few thinning strands of hair brushed over a pink scalp. His eyes were blue, watery and curious.

'There was a matter you wished to see me about?' asked the man, who had to be Amos Blount. He did not give his name, nor did he offer his hand.

'I represent the Double M ranch,' Tango replied, which was stretching the truth to its limit.

'The Double M?' the man looked truly perplexed, 'I thought . . . perhaps we had better step into my office,' the fat man said. Tango followed him to the rear of the bank, the cashier's still-suspicious eyes following them.

'Please take a seat,' Blount said, waving a hand around the small cluttered office where half a dozen wooden chairs with green leather pads rested on the uncarpeted floor. He seated himself behind his desk, almost every inch of which was littered with stacks of papers. 'Now then, Mr . . .'

'Tango. Drew Tango.'

'Mr Tango,' the little man said, steepling his fingers, leaning farther across his desk. 'What is this about? I was given to understand that Frank Baker was handling matters for the Double M.'

'That's just the point,' Tango said, bluffing his way into things. 'Mr Madison has lost faith in Baker's ability to handle his affairs.'

'Oh, I see! I was told that Kent Madison was on his deathbed.'

Tango managed a rueful smile. 'Baker tells a lot of people that. It isn't true. Mr Madison has been ill, but he

24

is recovering now.'

The banker looked pained. The twinkle left his eyes. 'I don't know what we can do about the deposit into Baker's account. I mean, the money came directly from Gage and Company. It's not like the bank is involved with that side of things.'

Tango continued to bluff. 'Did Mr Gage himself authorize the payment?'

'Oh, yes. Yes, Wesley Gage came here in person along with his associate, a Mr Craig?'

'This Mr Gage, did he give the impression of . . . well, does he resemble a walrus?'

Unexpectedly the banker broke out in a tittering laugh. Nodding his head he said, 'Yes, yes as a matter of fact! Although it's not polite to say so – we all have our physical flaws.'

'And the other one, he was a nervous little man with a thin mustache?'

'Yes, that was the man calling himself Mr Craig.' The banker regained his more serious tone of voice. 'Why do you ask? If you have reason to believe they were impostors. . . .'

'No, no,' Tango assured the banker. 'I just wanted you to confirm their descriptions. After meeting him once, they never returned to talk to Mr Madison again. He was beginning to assume that the deal had fallen through. Then I found out that Baker was trying to do all of the negotiating in his name. That's why I'm here. Roberta Madison doesn't want her father to find out what Baker has been up to. Mr Madison is getting better, but she fears a set-back if he were to discover what Baker has been trying to do.'

25

'I see,' the banker said, drumming his stubby fingers on the desk to. 'What do you suggest we do then, Mr, Tango?'

'Does Gage still intend to follow through with his arrangement?' Tango asked, still fishing for information.

'Oh, yes! They really want that timber from Mammoth Peak. I just don't know now what we can do, but if Mr Madison has been misinformed. . . .'

'I'll straighten that out with him,' Tango promised, rising. 'But I think you should consider deeply before conducting further business with Frank Baker.'

'Yes, yes I see,' Blount said, also rising. Now he did offer his hand and Tango shook it and departed, leaving a concerned Amos Blount behind.

The streets were bright with midday sunlight, hot with midday heat as Tango started uptown to look for Sparky. Well, the morning had been spent productively. He had discovered what Baker was up to. He was selling the timber up on Mammoth Point to these lumbermen. Of course he figured to get away with it. Kent Madison was in no condition even to ride his land to check it over. Roberta rode every morning, but across cattleland, not in the rugged country up along the slopes of Mammoth Point.

Frank Baker might have gotten away with it if the loggers meant to take the timber down the far slope, away from the ranch, which they undoubtedly did. The slope was less tricky, and Little Legend Creek flowed there toward the south-east, making transport less of a problem than wagoning the felled trees.

No one would have ever known. The ranch hands were busy bunching the cattle down in the valley and were preparing for a month-long drive to market. But four men had seen Baker with Gage and Craig. Not that they would

26

have suspected anything either, if Baker hadn't panicked and fired the four of them.

But Baker had been found out, and something had to be done about it. Roberta and Kent Madison had to be informed about the timber sale. He wished that he could have told Dane what they had found before he and Leland rode down to try to see the old man and have their conversation, but things never go exactly to plan in this life, as Tango well knew. He tugged his hat lower and strode along the plankwalk lending to the dingy little saloon where Sparky had decided to begin his own investigation.

When Bill Sparks had approached the Dos Picas saloon he had seen the usual assortment of horses hitched there: some rough-coated, some sleek and young; squat little Indian ponies and some remarkable animals, long-legged and deep-chested.

Four remarkable animals. These stood flecked with foam in the heated sunlight. One of them, a big gray, was quivering. Sparky frowned. Their owners had been so eager to quench their thirst inside the saloon that they had ignored the fact that a horse gets just as thirsty as a man. They should have been properly cooled, led to shade and watered. A man does that first. After all, what use was a man in the west without a horse?

Sparky felt an ill-defined anger rise within himself: ill-defined because he did not know who the men were, but they were torturing the animals through sheer neglect or stupidity. Sparky cared for horses as he cared for dogs and other living things. There were even a few of the female species that he had cared about in his short life. One of these last was the reason he was now living on the desert, homeless and broke. He was constantly working to convince himself that Shar was not worth the caring, and having little success at it even after all this time.

Sparky ran his hand gently over the gray horse's muzzle and then tramped into the saloon.

The place was vaguely cool, musty with the smell of stale beer and sawdust; it had a very low ceiling, a scattering of round wooden tables and flimsy-appearing chairs. Behind the dark, scarred bar a man in an apron stood wiping glasses with a cloth. The room was not crowded. Two older men sat hunkered in a corner, sharing a pitcher of beer. Along the bar four men stood in line, boots propped upon the brass rail. The owners of the four hard-ridden horses.

They were trail-dusty and bulky. Big shoulders and bearded faces caused them all to look similar. They swallowed their beer without talking to each other. Sparky felt like approaching them about their horses, but they undoubtedly knew what they had done and just did not care. It's not a good idea anyway, to approach strangers with criticism. Much as Sparky wanted to say something, he knew that it would do no good. It was not his place to comment.

From the looks of them they could easily beat him to a pulp if stirred up.

He decided to settle in at the far end of the bar and drink a beer himself while pondering his next move. He had hoped to find men talking, bragging, laughing about some small success or inflated wealth. Someone, that is, who knew the secret of Frank Baker and the two unknown city men who had been holding a secret meeting with the Double M foreman. It seemed now that this was not going to happen, not in this saloon, not on this day.

The two old, whiskered men still sat in the corner with their pitcher of beer, the four strange riders continued to drink in near silence at the bar.

Sparky was ready to give it up. Maybe Tango had had some luck at the hotel. Then, from the other end of the bar, someone growled:

'What are you looking at? You, Red!'

Sparky was the only man standing at the bar. He recognized the words as one of the oldest belligerent challenges in the world, one common to troublemakers everywhere.

'Everybody's got to be looking at something,' Sparky answered, trying for a smile.

'You don't have to be looking at me!' the bearded man replied, slapping his beer mug down heavily. Two of his friends smirked. The other continued to drink with no expression at all on his face.

The bully stepped away from the bar and glowered down its length. He was the smallest of the four bearded strangers; he was not quite as big as a bear. Sparky turned his options around in his mind and decided that the best tactic was simply to leave.

'Sorry I don't have the time to talk,' he said, finishing his beer and placing the mug down. He started toward the door and the big man deliberately placed his massive body in Sparky's way.

'You haven't apologized yet,' the stranger growled, his scowl deepening. The man, Sparky saw now, had managed to get himself pretty drunk, pretty quickly. Red eyes scoured Sparky's. 'Or would you prefer to fight it out?'

'Knock it off, Hummel,' one of the other strangers said.

'And just take whatever he says?'

'He hasn't said anything – we don't need trouble in this

29

hick town.'

Hummel hadn't finished. The man was a brute, his entertainment probably usually consisted of getting drunk and beating people up. At least, that was what he seemed to want for this morning's entertainment.

The door beyond the big man's back opened and a slash of yellow daylight painted the sawdust-strewn floor of the bar. The tall man entered, glancing one way and the other as his eyes adjusted to the relative darkness of the saloon's interior.

'Ready to go, Sparky?' Tango asked.

Sparky answered, 'I'm ready, but I seem to have myself in some kind of a bind.'

'Oh?' Tango looked along the bar, at the angry man who now turned toward him, and his hand lowered to dangle loosely new his holstered Colt.

'You keep out of this,' Sparky's antagonizer warned. One of the men at the bar, the one who had spoken earlier grabbed Hummel's arm.

'Why, you darned fool! Don't you know who that is? It's Drew Tango, or am I wrong?'

'You're not wrong,' Tango answered coldly.

'Is this sprout a friend of yours, Tango?'

'He is.'

'I suggest you get him out of here.'

'That's what I intend to do – one way or the other,' Tango said, his eyes now fixed on Hummel. 'Come on, Sparky. It's time to go.'

Sparky sidled past Hummel and Tango and made it to the door. Tango backed out of the saloon. Hummel had to be restrained by two of his friends, but perhaps that was part of the show. He did not follow Sparky and Tango out into the street.

'What did you do to make the big man so mad?' Tango asked as they tramped down the plankwalk toward Tonio's stable.

'Not a thing,' Sparky said, glancing back toward the saloon nervously.

'I didn't think so – I know his kind. Walk into a saloon often enough and you'll meet one of them.'

'I think I could have. . . .' Sparky began, then belatedly he said, 'Thanks, Tango.'

As they saddled their horses in Tonio's stable Sparky asked, 'Did you have any luck?'

'Quite a bit, as it happens,' Tango said, tightening the girths on his saddle. 'I'll tell you about it on the trail. I think we need to get back to the Double M as soon as possible. Those four men,' he told Sparky, 'I'd bet they're the men Baker hired to replace us – and I think we'll be meeting them again.'

THREE

Dane Hollister approached the white two-story frame house which was the home of Kent Madison, owner of the Double M ranch, and his daughter, Roberta, with some trepidation, It wasn't fear of being shot down by Frank Baker and whoever else he might have riding with him now, or of visiting Kent Madison in his sickbed, for Madison had always been kind and generous in his dealings with Dane.

It wasn't that simple. Dane was wary of meeting Roberta Madison. That slender, dark-eyed young woman was the girl of his dreams and Dane had always tried to impress her as a courageous, loyal and, most of all, well-mannered hand. She had never revealed anything close to a romantic interest in Dane, but a man always has hopes. He wondered now as he rode through the yard toward the back of the house whether Frank Baker had managed somehow to convince Roberta that there was a streak of evil in Dane Hollister. Somehow poisoned her opinion of Dane. The lies that had been spread about him caused Dane to begin to develop some doubts of his own. Had he ever gone too far in his admiration of Roberta? It seemed impossible, but perhaps once or twice without recalling it, he had said a word or two too many.

No matter; it was more important to speak to Kent Madison just then. Dane had not wanted to leave his horse in front of the house in full view, so he had chosen the kitchen entrance. Leland had been posted in the shade of the dusty live oak trees a little distant from the yard. He was to watch for Baker and fire a single shot if the ranch manager arrived. That should give Dane enough time to leave the house by the back. He did not intend to get into a shooting dispute with Baker.

At least, not until he had things sorted out with Kent Madison.

Dane swung down from his lazy old buckskin horse – the animal still needed to be spurred to run flat out, it plainly didn't like to exert itself – loosely hitched the horse and tramped up the swaying wooden steps toward the open kitchen door.

Carlos and Rita Real were both at work in the kitchen. Brother and sister, they were both small, energetic and capable. There the resemblance ended. Carlos could always be counted on for a smile, an offer of something to eat, a friendly word or two. Rita Real was cold as ice. Dane did not know whether she did not like him, the ranch or humanity in general. She had furry eyebrows and the shadow of a mustache She also had a violent temper, usually well concealed, but sometimes vented on her amiable brother when she thought no one was around.

'Dane!' Carlos said, turning from a large zinc washtub where dishes soaked. He wiped his hands on his apron and offered to shake with Dane. 'I thought you were gone! They say you rode out angry.'

'I came back,' Dane said. There was no point in trying to explain matters with a few words. Rita was preparing food on the counter across the room. She darted one venomous glance at Dane and continued with her work, dicing onions.

'I need to see Mr Madison,' Kent said, lowering his voice. Carlos frowned.

'I don't know, Dane. No one goes up there. Miss Roberta says—'

'You can't see him. Go!' Rita said without turning to face Dane. Her long knife continued to flicker and chop, thudding against the cutting-board.

'I only need a few minutes, you see—'

'A few minutes for what?' the voice in the doorway leading to the front room beyond asked. Dane turned his eyes that way to see Roberta Madison, glowing with morning freshness, wearing a white dress with small yellow flowers woven into the fabric. Dane removed his hat.

'I want to talk to your father,' he said.

'I don't think that's a good idea,' Roberta Madison said. Her eyes, her expression were enigmatic.

'Can you ask him? Please! It's important. It's ranch business, Ro— Miss Madison.'

She wavered, trying to make a decision. The doctor had instructed her to leave her father at peace, without disturbing news. This, from the expression on Dane's face, promised to be disturbing. The dark-haired man with his penetrating, professorial eyes, seemed over-eager. And vaguely appealing.

'I'll see if he's awake. Then I'll ask him if he will see you,' Roberta said. She turned away quickly and he could hear the heels of her small boots clacking on the stairs

34

leading to the second story.

Dane couldn't take the hostility in the kitchen, so he smiled at Carlos and left, walking into the front room with its massive stone fireplace, the rifles hanging on the wall beside a huge elk head which watched him stonily with its glass eyes. There was a large braided rug on the polished wood floor, a pair of brown leather couches facing each other across a wide space, two leather chairs seemingly arranged arbitrarily, and a small round mahogany table in one corner holding a large glass vase bright with newly picked summer wildflowers. Golden poppies, blue lupine and some flowers he didn't recognize immediately. He had started that way to examine the bouquet curiously when footsteps on the staircase caused him to halt and turn.

'Father would be pleased to see you,' Roberta said. 'but please keep it as brief as possible. He isn't getting any stronger.'

'I will try be keep my visit short.'

'Please do,' Roberta said, but then a passing shadow of regret moved across her dark eyes. Dane was taken upstairs and down the corridor to the bedroom where the former king of the Double M lay on his back in a massive four-poster bed. Heavy furniture was everywhere, high-backed chairs, a sturdy dresser and tall commode with an oval mirror, all of dark wood in the Spanish style. The only thing that was not sturdily carved lay in the bed. Dane had known that Madison was very ill, but it was a shock to see this white-haired man, his flesh shrunken over his bones.

When Dane had first come West, Madison had been full in the chest, broad-shouldered and powerful; astride a

35

massive gray horse, he had seemed to dwarf the other men around him. Now he lay, his eyes struggling to focus, gnarled, blue-veined hands twitching as he plucked aimlessly at his coverlet. His mouth moved in what might have been an attempted smile and eventually he spoke with the creaking sound of an opening coffin.

'Dane. Sit down, my boy. They haven't let me see anyone lately, said it was best for me. What can be so good about lying here lonely, uninformed and sick?'

'You're looking well, Mr Madison,' Dane said, dragging one of the heavy, high-backed chairs nearer the bed.

'Don't try to comfort me, Dane. I could see the shock on your face. It's of no importance. Tell me what brings you here.'

'It's in the nature of a grievance. I suppose you'd call it that,' Dane said, noticing that Roberta showed disapproval. Her small mouth tightened. He understood; she did not want her father upset, and here was Dane was doing exactly that.

'Grievance? Aren't the boys being fed well?' Kent Madison asked.

'They were the last I heard,' Dane said, hunching forward in his chair. 'I've been let go, you see.'

'You, Dane?' Madison's eyes showed concern. Dane had always been one of his favorites, a loyal rider, a hard worker.

'It's not just me, sir, or I wouldn't have come. Leland and Sparky were also fired. And Tango.'

'Tango!' Madison looked truly upset now. Roberta moved forward as if she might put a halt to the visit. 'Why, Tango is the heart and soul – the nerve – of Double M.'

'I agree with you, sir.'

36

'But what reason did Baker give? What were you four up to?'

Dane explained briefly about the accusations Baker had made about Leland and Sparky. 'Tango was given no reason for his dismissal – I suspect Baker didn't have the heart to face him. As for me,' Dane shot a glance at Roberta, 'I was told that your daughter complained to him that I was making unwanted advances toward her.'

Roberta's face briefly colored. Crab-apple-sized spots of red flushed her cheeks. 'I said no such thing to Baker or to anyone else,' she said firmly. 'It is a plain lie!'

Madison looked shocked, stunned, his pallid face paled even more. He was having trouble staying awake. His pupils were dilated, his hands twitched. Dane felt suddenly ashamed of himself for having carried bad news to Kent Madison, a man who had virtually saved his own life when he had agreed to hire on Dane, an inexperienced cowhand, at Double M.

'It's a little too much,' Madison said, and then his legs began to twitch beneath the covers. It was a violent, short-lived movement which caused Dane to frown and simultaneously to rise at Roberta Madison's silent urging.

They walked together out into the corridor and Roberta closed the door gently behind them.

'He's being poisoned, you know,' Dane said.

'He can't be!' Roberta said with astonishment.

'I'm almost certain. The dilated pupils, the sudden uncontrollable motions of his limbs, the following lethargy. Yes, Roberta, I think he is being slowly poisoned to death.'

'But who, how. . . ?' Roberta could not accept the idea. She shook her head, bit at her lower lip, searched Dane's

37

eyes with her own liquid gaze. 'The doctor didn't think. . . .'

'The doctor hasn't spent as much time on the range as I have. Perhaps he simply couldn't accept the possibility himself but I know what I am seeing. When I was. . . .' Dane nearly went on to speak of his days in medical school, but he did not.

'What could it be?' Roberta asked in confusion.

'Do you know what jimson weed is?'

'Yes, I think so – that little plant with the purple flowers. Don't they call it loco weed, too?'

'Sometimes, although there are different plants called loco weed. Jimson is very toxic. Cattle graze on it because they know no better and after a while they become unsteady in their movements – their legs twitch violently. Eventually they die if they ingest enough of it. There was time when some of the desert Indians used to make tea from jimson for some of their religious ceremonies. They, however, knew the dangers and how to control the potency. Ranchers destroy jimson whenever, wherever it is found growing.'

'But how can you. . . ?'

'The flowers downstairs, the ones near the door. Where did they come from?'

'I don't see what . . . Rita picked them; she brings in a new bouquet every morning,' Roberta told him.

'There's jimson-weed flowers among them,' Dane said. 'Their leaves have been stripped off.'

Roberta was shocked. The fingers of both hands went to her lips. 'You can't think that Rita. . . ?'

'Just now I don't think anything as to who is doing it, I'm just saying that I'm sure of what is causing your father's deterioration. What I want you to do, Roberta,' he said, and yielding to impulse, he took her small hands in his own, 'is to not let your father have any sort of tea, no special meals. Serve him what the other men on the ranch are having to eat. It may be plainer fare, but it will be healthier.'

'But Dane,' Roberta said, her dark eyes remaining fixed on his, 'if what you say is true—'

A rifle shot sounded outside the house, not too distant. 'I have to go now,' he said. 'There's trouble afoot. I just wanted you and your father to know that. I can't stop to talk more now.'

In response to Leland's signal, Dane half-ran, half-slid down the staircase and darted through the kitchen which now held only a startled Carlos Real, up to his elbows in dishwater. Dane was into the saddle of his buckskin in minutes, touching the tips of his rowels to the horse's flanks to prove he was not kidding about needing some speed.

Dane made it to the grove of oak trees, drawing no fire. He did not look behind him as he emerged, to find Toby Leland riding with his rifle still in hand, dust streaming out behind him. They were already out of sight of the house, so they slowed by mutual consent and cooled their horses as they continued on their way.

'Well?' Dane asked at length as they rounded a jumbled stack of yellow boulders which rose a hundred feet into the hot, dusty air. Beyond these the Yavapai Range rose in folded, gray confusion, deep shadows slashing their flanks, brilliant sunlight reflecting off mica and quartz deposits along their ridges.

'It was Baker,' Toby Leland said, panting as if he and

39

not his roan horse had run from the ranch. 'Him and four other men. I was hoping you'd have time to get out of there. Otherwise. . . .'

'Otherwise we would have had to do a little shooting,' Dane said. 'Did you recognize the men with him?'

'They were too far away: but they didn't look like anyone I know.'

'Probably our replacements,' Dane said.

'I suppose,' Leland answered with a weary nod. 'Did you have any luck at the house?'

'Some.' Dane proceeded to tell the younger man what had happened inside the Madison house.

'I knew Kent Madison didn't know anything about us being fired!' Leland nearly shouted.

'No, but there's little he can do about it now,' Dane said. 'He isn't strong at all.'

'They can't have been poisoning him,' Leland said with deep distress. To the young ranch hand that seemed a hundred times more despicable than simply shooting a man dead. 'Are you sure?'

'He showed all the signs of poisoning,' Dane answered with a quick shake of his head, 'Am I entirely certain? No, but I'd bet the farm on it – had I a farm to bet.'

'Beats me why they're doing all of this,' Leland said, still morose as they turned their ponies toward Rose Canyon. 'Who profits anything from Madison's death? Outside of Roberta, that is. . . ?' Leland glanced at Dane and clamped his mouth shut. He knew he had said the wrong thing. Dane's face grew briefly stony and then softened again; Leland was only thinking out loud.

'If Baker has Kent Madison out of the way, all sorts of mischief could be tried. There's a herd of five hundred steers there, waiting to be driven to market. That's a fair amount of money on the hoof, enough to tempt a dishonest man. Roberta hasn't the strength to fight them off, if that's what they're up to, and none of us is around any more to help her. The rest of the boys on Double M are all right, but they'll be hitting the trail soon with the herd.'

'Did you happen to remember to ask Roberta about how Calvin McGraw really died, as Tango suggested?'

'I remembered,' Dane said, 'but it was about then that you fired that warning shot. It will have to wait for another time.'

'As I remember,' Leland said, 'it was always told that McGraw was just old and sick. Do you think he was poisoned too, Dane?'

'I don't think we'll ever know,' Dane answered as they found the mouth of Rose Canyon and started their ponies upward into its dusty, shadowed reaches. 'We can only deal with what we know now, which is very little.'

'Almost nothing,' Leland agreed. 'Let's hope that Tango and Sparky found out something about those two citified strangers.'

'Let's hope so,' Dane replied. Then he fell into a prolonged thoughtful silence as they rode their horses deeper into the canyon which bulked on either side of them, cutting off sunlight and cooling breeze alike. It was a lost and desolate place for a man's last refuge.

FOUR

'Timber!' Dane Hollister exclaimed after Tango had told them what he had discovered in Dos Picos. 'Is that what this is all about?'

'So it seems,' Tango replied. He was perched on a low flat rock, hat tilted back, staring at the cold fire-pit. They had all agreed that it was not a good idea to start a fire in the present circumstances. Dace pressed Tango to tell his story again in case he had missed something, so Tango told him about the meeting with the banker, Amos Blount, about verifying that the two men they had seen up along Mammoth Point were from the Gage Lumber Company, and that the company had deposited an unspecified amount of money into the bank for Frank Baker.

'That's all you could find out?' Leland asked.

'That's about all there is to it. Baker sold the rights to that high country timber to Gage and Company, accepted payment for it and has since been trying to keep anyone from discovering the sale.'

'Which is probably why they've been trying to keep Kent Madison as incapacitated as possible,' Dane said. 'He used to like long rides, enjoyed circling every inch of the ranch. He would have found out.'

'But Roberta might never have. I can't see her riding up that far north for any reason.'

'Neither can I,' Dane had to admit. Her idea of a good recreational ride was to cover a few miles of flat grazing land, not to negotiate those tricky mountain roads. 'At first I thought that Baker must be after the cattle, this being round-up time, but stolen cows would be harder to sell – you can't brand a pine tree. The four men in the saloon, Tango? Did you recognize any of them?'

'One of them was called Hummel,' Sparky remembered.

'I recognized Jeb Fry,' Tango said with a frown. He rose and stretched his back muscles. Dane was disturbed by the mention of Fry. His face was lined with concern. The two younger men had never heard of Jeb Fry, and looked at each other in puzzlement. Tango told them:

'Fry was serving five years in Yuma prison for a little dust-up down South. He was sentenced for assault on an officer of the law – the county sheriff. The assault was putting a bullet into the man. It must have been one of Fry's off days. The man lived.'

No one asked how Tango had gotten this information; the two younger hands were learning better. Dane accepted the statement as fact. Sparky grew suddenly animated.

'You should have seen how Tango backed those boys down. . . .' Then he was silent again. Tango had shot him the briefest of scathing glances and Sparky buried his enthusiasm.

'Now what do we do?' Leland wanted to know. 'We know what's going on, we know who's behind it, we know that Baker has brought in some hardcases to keep the timbermen from being interfered with. But . . . what can we do now?'

Everyone looked to Dane Hollister for the answer, but he too rose to his feet to stretch, and simply said, 'I think we'd better try to get some rest for now, and I believe we might be well-served if we took turns standing guard down the canyon. I don't know yet what we should do, but I have a pretty good idea what Frank Baker will try if he discovers our camp. We have advertised that we're still in the area: Sparky and Tango in Dos Picos; me at the Madison house. They'll be on the lookout for us, boys, that much is certain.'

'I'll take first watch,' Toby Leland volunteered. He hadn't had a long ride as Sparky and Tango had, and he was the youngest of them, still energetic and full of enthusiasm.

Dane Hollister rolled up in his blankets as the desert night settled, chilling them. Dane was not so much feigning sleep as fighting it off. They had themselves a large problem now, and he was not sure how to approach it, so he had cut off the inquiries from the others who constantly looked to him for answers. As if he had any for them. As if he even had any for himself.

He tried to think of Roberta Madison and carry thoughts of her gentle beauty into his dreams, but that only added to his problems. He could not sleep or dream of her, knowing that even now she was probably in danger from Frank Baker who would not hesitate to strike once he thought that his plan to steal the timber from Mammoth Point was discovered. Baker was not the type of man who would give up on his scheme easily. Dane Hollister made his decision.

'Tango?' he whispered, 'are you awake? I think we have to go after Frank Baker.'

'I agree,' Tango's muffled voice answered from beneath his blanket.

'Sooner rather than later,' Dane said.

'I agree. Now let me get some sleep.'

Dane smiled at Tango in the darkness, then rose and strapped on his gun-belt. He might as well relieve Leland, who was standing watch. There would be no sleep for Dane Hollister on this star-bright, savage night.

As was his habit, Tango was first to rise in the morning even though he had taken over from Dane in standing watch at midnight. Tango usually slept well; it was only when the dawn hour approached that his old demons came, back tormenting him. It was impossible to go back to sleep after he started thinking about his long past trails littered with ghosts, so he had long ago decided it was better just to rise and face the new day, no matter what demons it might have lurking.

Walking to the headwaters, Tango again washed off. The water was ice-cold, the air around him night-cooled. It was hard to believe that within three hours the desert floor would be heated to three-digit numbers. Rose Canyon held the chill of night for quite a while; its high bluffs preventing the gorge from receiving sunlight before then, but at midday it was a furnace and, just as it held the chill of night, so it also emitted the heat of day long after sunset.

Had it not been for the spring, no one, not even the ancient Yavapai Indians could have endured dwelling long in its curiously twisted, barren depths. That was irrelevant:

45

they were here and here they would stay unless pried out or until they had determined to sally out to make war. There was little chance of them being uprooted; anyone riding toward them through the mouth of the canyon would be seen and met with gunfire, and there was no way to scale the bluffs looming overhead.

But it meant, of course, that there was no secret way for them to escape if they were discovered. All Frank Baker would need to do was post a guard, a besieging army below and wait until hunger or the exigency of sheer deprivation drove them from their sanctuary.

Tango was thinking along these lines as he swept his damp hair back and planted his hat, buttoning the snaps on his faded blue shirt. Dane was right – remaining in the canyon like cowering animals was no good. They had to go on the offensive against Baker and his mob of assembled gunmen.

These they knew little about. Of the four, they had identified two. Hummel was apparently a bully, given to wild bursts of anger. Jeb Fry, whom Tango knew too well, was cool and deliberate in his actions. At the time when Jeb was locked up in Yuma Prison Tango had known the man, but only to nod to in passing, One story that was passed around about Fry was that he had once, on a bet, dueled with a roughneck named Kyper. At a distance of fifty paces Fry, it was said, had shot the nose off his opponent, Some bystanders had taken it for a missed shot, but it turned out that Jeb Fry had made a bet that he could do just that, and that the bet was the reason behind the duel.

It might have been true, it might not. You heard a lot of wild stories in the West. Yet there was no denying that Fry was a superior marksman, and a cold-hearted gunman.

Two men flanked the still-cold fire-pit when Tango returned to the camp: Leland and Dane Hollister. Sparky was standing watch, although that would soon become pointless. In daylight they would see and hear anyone approaching their camp. Tango mentioned this and sent Leland off to bring Sparky in so that they could all confer on what to do.

Tango crouched down and asked Dane, 'Any ideas on how to go about this?'

'First we have to decide what out real objective is, Tango. Do we want to get even with Baker, protect the Double M, chase off the loggers coming to Mammoth Point?'

Tango didn't look up as he answered, 'Yes.'

'All of those,' Dane smiled. 'I like the way you think, Tango.' He went on, 'Then I think we have to decide on a plan of operations. For example, could we possibly recruit Gomez, Allison, Sully and Kramer to the cause? That would give us a two-to-one advantage.'

'Do we want to drag them into this?' Tango asked. 'They're all good, hard-working ranch hands, but do you want to ask them to take a bullet for our cause? Plus, Dane, the herd is nearly ready for a trail drive. If that bunch of cows doesn't get to market, Kent Madison and his daughter won't have any income for another year. I say we leave the other hands out of this.'

'I suppose you're right,' Dane answered grimly.

'My thinking is that we can ruin Baker's plans simply by stopping the Mammoth Point logging. We have to get up there and be ready to stand firm before the cutting begins.'

'The lumber company won't like it.'

47

'No, and they think they have signed a binding deal. That's just too bad. Let them sue Baker or have him thrown in prison.'

'Could be a couple of men killed along the way.'

'I know it,' Tango said, rising now to watch as Sparky and Leland walked back to camp, Sparky holding his rifle over his shoulder, gripping the barrel. These were his recruits against Baker and his contingent of toughs. He hated the thought of getting one of the youngsters killed, but he saw no other way. Dane would try it himself if he had to, for Kent Madison, for Roberta. Leland and Sparky had to be given the choice, told they might die. When they had all first gathered in the canyon, it had been the four of them against Frank Baker. The odds had changed dramatically.

'Let them make their own choice,' Dane said, as if reading Tango's mind. 'We'll just make it clear what is bound to happen from here on.'

'Why so glum!' Sparky asked, reaching the campsite, noticing the unsettled looks on the faces of Dane and Tango.

'We want to make sure you understand the turn things have taken,' Dane said.

'What? That Baker has brought in four bully boys?' Sparky said, as if it were of no concern to him.

'That, yes, and the fact that the timber company will bring its own hardmen in when they start to work.'

Leland locked uncertain. 'We're going to take them all on? Alone?'

'That's the way it's shaping up,' Dane said.

'How can we hope to—'

Sparky clapped his hand on his friend's shoulder.

48

'Don't worry, Leland. We're invincible.'

That's just it, Dane Hollister thought, we're not. It was only in books that the good men always won.

'We just want to be sure that you know what you're getting into,' Dane told them. 'If you want to pull out, it's all right. No one will fault you for it.'

'It's just. . . .' Leland hesitated. He was obviously considering the possibilities in a new light; the light of his own mortality. 'I mean, I owe Double M something, but. . . .'

'But not your life,' Dane said with an understanding nod.

'It's not that I'm afraid,' Leland said quickly, 'It's just that. . . .'

A new voice spoke up. Talking as they were, they had not heard the incoming rider.

'If you don't mind, men, I want to join your gang.' They turned to find themselves facing Roberta Madison.

Roberta sat beside Tango on that flat rock he used as a bench and she told them: 'Father passed away. It was a terrible death.' She had to pause and compose herself before she could go on. The men around her waited silently. She sniffed, dabbed at her nose with a small handkerchief and continued. 'Around midnight he started to twitch again, convulsively. His eyes rolled back in his head. There was foam on his lips. I don't know what sort of agony he must have been enduring. I screamed,' she admitted, shamefaced, 'because there was nothing I could do for him. It was so frustrating. My father was dying and I could do nothing!'

She composed herself again. The yellow sun, harsh and uncaring, had begun to show its face above the bluffs

49

surrounding the canyon. Shadows shortened rapidly. No man had spoken a word yet. Sitting there in her divided buckskin riding-skirt, white blouse and wearing a red scarf around her disarranged dark hair, she seemed small and vulnerable. Roberta dabbed at her nose again and wadded her handkerchief into a tight ball in her clenched hand.

'He was poisoned,' Dane Hollister commented. 'All of the symptoms were there. *Datura stramonium.*' The others gawked at him. Leland thought that Dane had been saying some sort of benediction. Dane lifted his eyes.

'Jimson weed,' he said, and now it was Roberta who narrowed her eyes. Dane certainly had not learned the Latin term for the plant on the range.

'Mr Hollister told me yesterday that he suspected poison. I believe now he was right,' Roberta said. 'That noxious little plant does have appealing blooms, but it has an unhealthy odor about it and I frequently wondered why Rita was bringing them into the house. I just thought she had a poor sense of smell. I opened the window in that corner and gave no more thought to it.'

'I want to say for all of us, Miss Madison, that we are truly sorry,' Tango told Roberta. 'He helped us all a little on this road of life.'

Roberta looked up, nodded, and then started to weep uncontrollably. Dane felt impelled to go to her and comfort her, but restrained himself. Sparky turned away. He could not stand the sight of a woman crying. When Shar— He had to force that thought aside roughly. After half a minute, Roberta composed herself and she apologized.

'I'm sorry, men, I couldn't help it.'

'No need for an apology,' Tango said. 'Even the rough-

est of men cries at some time in his life.' Roberta, Sparky
and Leland all glanced at Tango, wondering how he could
have ever been brought to tears, doubting it. Dane
Hollister only nodded. He knew well enough.

Roberta was not through with her story.

'In the morning I went downstairs to find Frank Baker
lounging around with four rough-looking men. They had
already started drinking whiskey and I told Frank: "My
father has passed away, and I am in no mood for company."

'He only looked at me and lifted one corner of his
mouth in a sneer. He did not move, he did not ask the
other men to go outside or to the bunkhouse and they for
their part seemed at home and content. One of the
men . . .' Roberta's voice broke a little, 'made a quite
callous remark about my father's death and then sugessted
I join him on the sofa for a drink.'

Dane Hollister's face was stony, the anger in his eyes was
clear to all. Tango scratched at his eyebrow and looked
away, Leland looked impotently enraged. Sparky said:

'I'll bet that was Hummel.'

'What did you do, Miss Madison?'

'What? I walked out through the kitchen and had
Gomez saddle my horse. Then I rode away without
looking back.'

'Was Rita there – in the kitchen?' Dane asked.

'She was there. She was smiling! She had a tray of fresh
drinks for Frank Baker and his men. I practically had to
shove her aside to get past her.'

'Miss Madison—' Dane began but she cut him off.

'Oh, for heaven's sake! Will everyone just call me
Roberta! I'm no longer boss lady of the Double M. I'm no
longer anything at all,' she said, then despite herself she

began to cry again.

'It's only temporary,' Tango said in a quiet voice. 'We'll have Baker out of your house and off your land in no time.'

Roberta looked around at their faces. Tango confident, Dane Hollister worried and angry, Sparky unreasonably sure of himself, Leland looking collapsed and frightened. She wanted to believe them, needed to, but it was hard to believe that the Rose Canyon gang could stand up to the men who had invaded her home.

'We'll fight for you, Miss . . . Roberta,' Sparky assured her cheerfully. 'You don't have a thing to worry about.'

That wasn't the way Dane Hollister would have said it. Of course he would fight for her, they all would, But as far as not having a thing to worry about – well, yes, she did. Losing her father, having a trail herd ready for market without an adequate crew or a reliable man in charge, the timber-poachers encroaching on her property up along Mammoth Point, her house invaded by a gang of thugs.

'Dane?' Sparky asked the man. Dane Hollister rose.

'Let's get started, men. No one ever won a battle just by the planning.'

FIVE

They rode off toward Mammoth Point. They agreed that was the place to start now, before the lumbermen had begun their work, when Baker had no known reason to ride up there himself. Although Dane, irrational as the impulse was, would have liked to ride to the Double M and just have it out with Frank Baker and his hired guns.

The day was hot, the trail dusty, as they climbed into the hills; the breeze was cut off by the scattered pines and occasional cedar tree. Silver squirrels mocked their slow progress, chattering and leaping from branch to branch, apparently only to demonstrate their own agility. Roberta was glum, Tango silent, Leland uneasy. Sparky did not display his usual high spirits. Dane rode with a single objective: to rid the Double M of the predators. Even the sight of Roberta's slim back as she sat her gray horse, her dark hair flying free, did little to raise his spirits.

He knew they were riding into serious trouble.

At the crest of the peak where they could look down and see the Little Legend Creek snaking its way southward like a silver snake through the pines, they paused for a while to let the horses blow. Dane drew up beside Tango and asked:

'See anyone?'

'No. I don't think that they've had time to organize a full crew and transport them up here yet.'

'It depends on how badly they want that timber.'

Tango nodded, There was little timber to be had in the Arizona Territory and some towns, like Phoenix and Tucson, were growing rapidly. New settlers were demanding more than adobe block structures and brick-making was not a strong industry west of the Mississippi. Gage and Craig must have congratulated themselves on pulling off such a coup. They would be enraged to find their plans flattened.

They couldn't have known they were buying rustled lumber – or could they?

'I think I see some movement far down the valley, near to the river,' Sparky said, squinting into the sun-bright distances. No one else could make out anything, anyone in that direction. After a while they started that way, winding down the slope where the trees themselves seemed to be panting for air. It was easily 100 degrees now; the scent of the pines was heightened by the temperature of the day. A woodpecker busy torturing a cedar tree was startled by their passing and winged low only inches from Roberta's face.

'Cheeky little thing,' Roberta said. Her attempt at humor was throttled by her obviously burdened thoughts. Her laugh was hollow. It fooled no one. Dane's heart was breaking for the woman; he wanted to ride near to her, to offer his strong arms to her, to let her finish with her mourning, but it was not the time, not the place.

'I see some people now,' Leland said and they slowed their horses even more.

Ahead, through the closing ranks of jack pines, they could see a group of men – four, six? – setting up camp not far from the river. Where they had come from there was no telling, but apparently they had arrived in canoes, for there were two of the craft beached not far from the camp. Dane saw a doe with its twin fawns approach the river and then back away out of caution. Above, the trees were dotted with black crows, cawing in apparent derision at the intruders in their domain.

'How do you want to do this, Dane?' Tango asked.

'We just march right up to them,' Roberta began, but Tango's eyes sent the message that he was asking Dane, and he wanted a cooler response.

'Maybe we should split up in case there is trouble,' Dane said. 'After all, these are only workmen who are doing what they've been asked to do for pay. Still, they won't be willing to leave on our say-so. Take Sparky and circle around to the north; we'll give you a few minutes to get into position.'

'All right,' Tango answered. Sparky, who had been listening, said:

'At last, some action,' with unwarranted enthusiasm. Toby Leland looked only doubtful.

Roberta Madison had fire in her eyes. She looked as if she were ready to bite someone. Her desperate anger had fixed on a target. This, she believed, she could do something about. It was not like watching her father die, the ranch being taken over. Here was a battle she could win. Dane Hollister wasn't so sure.

'Take it easy, Roberta. Until we see what their mood is. They've settled in for a long job. This will be like firing them from it on the day they start.'

'They have no right to start!' Roberta said grimly. 'The river is the northern boundary of the Double M.'

'These men probably don't know that. Their bosses sent them up here to work.' He looked pleadingly at her, 'Let's be careful.'

There was some disparaging criticism in her eyes as she looked directly into those of Dane. Roberta didn't realize that it was her safety that primarily concerned him. She might have taken his words of caution as signs of cowardice, and the implied criticism caused hot blood to flush his neck and cheeks.

'Tango's had enough time,' he said roughly. Then he slapped his buckskin's flanks with the ends of his reins and led Roberta and Leland forward into the lumber camp.

A man moving a heavy bundle from one of the canoes halted in mid-stride, dropped his parcel and reached for his rifle, which hung on a sling across his back. A second man near a still-cold fire stopped his work and stood with an axe in his hand. From across the camp a narrow man with a patch over his right eye stood, hands on his hips, watching their approach. A fourth man, a lumbering ox with the sleeves of his red-checked shirt rolled up over powerful forearms, simply stared expressionlessly at the three arriving riders.

The man with the patch over his eye made calming gestures and strode forward to meet them. His good eye had an expression that might have been humor or appreciation as it rested on Roberta Madison. Dane found that, unreasonably, he didn't care for either interpretation of the glance.

He was growing too possessive, with no particular encouragement from Roberta. He wondered vaguely

56

whether Frank Baker had detected the feeling that Dane had for Roberta and translated it into the charge he had made against Dane, knowing that it was at least half of the truth. The man with the eye patch now took the bridle to Roberta's gray horse, another move that Dane didn't care for, and spoke to Dane.

'Forgive the boys, They're a little jumpy. New country – they don't know if there's Indians about or not yet.'

'There aren't,' Dane told him.

'Well, that's good to hear. What are you folks doing way up here?' He asked the question casually, but Dane had the idea that he was taking their measure.

'You can't stay here!' Roberta burst out, no longer able to contain herself. 'Are you aware that this is Double M property?'

'Why, yes, miss, I am aware of that. I've got a plan of the area. That's why we're restricted to this side of the river. Double M, yes, miss. And we have the authorization of the owner to take timber here.'

'You do not!' Roberta said in a fiery voice. 'I am now the owner of the Double M.'

'It says here,' the man with the eyepatch said, taking a much-folded piece of yellow paper from his shirt pocket, 'that rights have been assigned by Mr Kent Madison, legal property owner of this land to—'

'Kent Madison is dead!' Roberta said, 'and besides, he never signed any such authorization.'

'Maybe you just weren't aware of it.'

Dane looked around. The other loggers were drawing closer, the one with his rifle, the big man now carrying an axe. A third wore a handgun in easy reach. There was no sign of Tango and Spark.

'I would have been aware of it,' Roberta said through her teeth. 'My father hadn't left his bed in over three months.'

'Then his representative—'

Roberta cut him off. 'He had no representative! Someone has tricked your Mr Gage.'

'Mr Gage doesn't make mistakes when it comes to legal matters,' the man said sharply. 'If there's a problem, take it up with him; leave us to our work.'

The man's attitude had hardened. Dane said, 'You're trespassing, mister.'

'Bring the law up here to tell us that,' the man with the eyepatch answered truculently. Now the other men had indeed closed a circle around them. Dane could see Leland fidgeting in his saddle, uncertain and unnerved.

'I'll tell you once again – you're trespassing. I'd advise you to pack up and get out of here.'

'Or you'll drive us off?' the timberman asked, looking at the three of them, then back toward his crew.

'If we're forced to,' Dane replied.

'I don't see how. . . .' the man with the patch said.

'Maybe you're just not looking close enough,' Tango's voice said as he and Sparky entered the camp on foot, both with their Colts drawn. Tango told Dane, 'I had the rest of the men hold back, see if this couldn't be done reasonably.'

'Thanks,' Dane said. 'I don't want there to be a blood-bath over a little misunderstanding.'

The man with the eyepatch had let go of Roberta's horse's bridle and was backing away, his face drawn taut. It wasn't clear whether he was more in fear of losing his job or his life, but he had lost his swagger. Unfortunately the big bull of a man with his axe in hand hadn't. He took three steps closer, the rifleman at his side.

'Why don't you just ride out of here, mister, before I do some harm to you and your woman?'

That was enough for Tango. Bracing himself in a dueling stance, he fired off and the bullet from his .44 severed the axe handle near the head, the steel falling to the ground. Tango's second shot flashed as the rifleman turned and tried to bring his long gun up to his shoulder. It tagged the logger in the knee and he went down howling with pain. Tango had shifted his sights to the third man who started to draw his own revolver, hesitated and then gave it up, seeing that he was too late in reacting.

'Maybe you do want to go back to Tucson and check with your boss,' Tango said, looking at the man with the eyepatch. The wounded logger continued to howl in pain. The big brutish lumberjack looked as if he would like to tear Tango's head off his neck, but he didn't have the nerve to make another move. He dropped the shattered handle of his axe and went to assist his injured friend.

'We're going,' the leader of the timber crew said to Dane, 'but we'll be back with more men – dozens of them, and if we find out you're running a bluff on us, it will take more than your hired gun there to hold us off.'

'Hired gun!' Sparky snorted as they watched the loggers limp away, carrying their wounded comrade. 'That was some shooting, though, Tango.'

Tango who only now holstered his gun after reloading two cartridges shook his head. 'Not my best day,' he said to Sparky as they went to retrieve their horses from the forest.

'The man with the axe. . . .' Sparky said excitedly.

'That was a good shot,' Tango agreed. 'But I shouldn't have aimed for it. As for the second shot, it was just bad.'

'What do you mean?' Sparky asked as he gathered up the reins to his little dun horse. 'You got him, didn't you? And with a snap shot at that.'

'I got him,' Tango said as he swung aboard his sorrel. His mouth was tight. 'But I shouldn't have hit him.'

'Why? I don't understand, Tango.'

Tango almost didn't answer, but he knew that Sparky had a true interest, so he told him: 'He was standing with his rifle low. He took it to his shoulder as I shot.'

'You were trying to hit his rifle!' Sparky asked, in awe.

'That's right. I didn't mean to hit the man, I got too cocky. That will get me killed some day.'

'But, Tango, if he was intending to shoot you, why. . . ?' They sat their ponies side by side in the dusty, shaded forest. It came to Sparky then. He said in a lower voice, 'You didn't want to kill a man again, did you?'

'No.' Tango turned his sorrel's head and started across the camp to join Dane, Roberta and Leland. Sparky followed slowly, his mind reflecting on other things that Tango had told him. The killing of the wrong man on the railroad. He knew that that was what Tango was remembering. And he knew that Tango was trying to cut it too fine – shooting at the weapons the men carried instead of using the entire target silhouette. And Sparky had to agree with what Tango had said: if he kept on doing that he was going to miss one day and it would leave Tango dead.

It was a fine sense to have the death of a man, even your worst enemy in mind, but not if it cost you your own life.

They rode the long road to the back of the ridge known as

Mammoth Point. In other parts of the country – Colorado for instance, where the peaks soared to 14,000 feet and higher – the idea of calling a squat, crumbling ridge by a name like 'Mammoth' would have seemed absurd. But for southern Arizona, the peak was considered large. It had once, in years past, even gotten snowfall and held it for all of a week.

'Well, we showed them,' Sparky heard Roberta saying. 'They won't be back, no matter what the one-eyed man was saying.'

Sparky did not believe that, nor did Dane Hollister from the expression he was wearing. Gage Lumber Company had invested a lot in that timber – how much was uncertain – and they were not going to be backed off a claim they believed to be legitimate. Roberta was going to have to get some legal help with matters. Surely Gage and Craig would be outraged by this and seek out their own lawyer or judge, possibly a United States marshal to look into matters. Roberta would have to have her position clarified legally, except that now with Kent Madison dead, unable to testify, his will probably in probate, no one would be able to prove that a sick old man had not somehow been persuaded to agree to terms with the timber company.

They had a long way to go.

Running off four men who were only setting up a base camp for the arriving loggers would achieve nothing more than infuriating Gage. However, Sparky held his tongue as did Dane Hollister, who let Roberta enjoy her brief moment of triumph.

'What now?' Sparky asked as he rode beside Dane Hollister, who seemed disgruntled. Roberta had slowed

61

her pony to ride alongside Tango. Maybe that had something to do with Dane's mood.

'Roberta has to get the legal side of this straightened out or the loggers will just come back again and again. It has to be shown that Kent Madison had not assigned timber rights, could not have and that Frank Baker was falsely representing himself as Dent's agent.'

'Think it can be done?' Sparky asked.

'Of course it can, but it might be a lengthy legal battle. In the meantime the law can order Gage Lumber Company to stay off the property until there is a decision.'

'So Roberta has to go to Dos Picos?'

'The sooner the better,' Dane said. 'She can also begin prosecution against Baker.'

'You'll be riding with her, I suppose?'

'No,' Dane said in annoyance. 'Tango had better go. He has already introduced himself as the Double M representative. The banker knows him. It's less messy if they maintain that fiction. Besides, Tango might have to defend himself concerning the shooting of the Gage lumberjack. It's better if he and Roberta report the incident first, rather than wait for Gage to file a complaint about him.'

'Us,' Sparky asked, nodding toward a somber Leland, 'what are we going to do, Dane?'

Dane sighed. He had thought this through along the trail and believed there was only one course of action. 'If Baker has a hint that he has failed in selling the timber up on Mammoth, he might decide to take the only other asset he has in hand and turn it over into ready cash.'

'The cattle?' Sparky responded.

'The cattle. He's still got five hundred beeves on the

hoof. If he gets word that the timber deal might fall through, he can still drive them to the trailhead and sell them. It would be simple: he's got half of the old crew and his new hires, the cattle are already bunched and he has a buyer waiting for them.'

Sparky grinned unexpectedly.

'What is it?' Dane asked. He was in no mood for humor.

'Nothing, except that I don't think those four hired guns are expecting to be put to work herding cattle on the long trail. Somehow I can't see Hummel or Jeb Fry being happy about actually having to do some work with their hands that doesn't involve their trigger fingers.'

'Well, it hasn't happened yet. I'm thinking we three ought to hole up in the canyon again and draw matches to see who is going to ride down to the ranch and try to talk to Gonzales and the other men in the bunkhouse. They deserve to be warned.'

'No sense drawing matches,' Sparky said after yawning. 'Look, Dane, you and Leland have already been down to the ranch. You, they saw – or at least Rita and Carlos saw you. Someone may have spotted Leland as well, or at least recognized his horse. I figure it has to be me. I drag in begging for my old job back. Maybe Baker throws me off the ranch; it doesn't matter, I'll find a way to talk to some of the men and let them know what's happening, what has been done to Miss Roberta.'

'All right,' Dane said after a thoughtful minute. 'I suppose you're right. I only wish it could be me.' He seemed to be speaking of returning to the ranch, yet his eyes were fixed on Roberta and Tango, discussing matters between themselves. What Dane was wishing was plain in his expression. He wished he were the one riding to Dos

63

Picos with Roberta Madison.

When they neared the mouth of Rose Canyon again it was midday and hot as a firecracker. They halted in a group in the shade of the northern bluff. 'You two had better proceed to Dos Picos as soon as possible,' Dane told them, speaking to Tango and Roberta. 'We'll sit here a while to make sure that no one is following.'

'Then?' Tango asked.

'We're going to try to pry some of the hands – Gomez, Allison and the others – free of Baker. He'll have a tough enough time driving that herd with the men he has; we can weaken him even further.'

'Do you want me to do something – write a note, perhaps?' Roberta asked.

'That's a fine idea,' Dane said. 'Rather than having the men think that we just might be disgruntled employees.'

Dane, who always carried a pencil, dug for it in his saddle-bags, offering the stubby implement to Roberta. For paper he tore a flyleaf from a small blue-bound book he had been reading. Roberta had noticed the title and author. 'That new author, Emily Dickinson,' she said. 'Have you been reading her poetry?'

'Yes,' Dane answered, handing her the blank page. 'A very lonely woman, it seems to me.'

Whatever Dane had meant to convey to Roberta, he got no reaction. Roberta finished signing her note and handed it to Dane who passed it off to Sparky.

'Let's hit the trail,' Tango said. Roberta nodded and they started away from the Rose Canyon gang, lining their ponies out toward Dos Picos.

'Why don't you give the man a break?' Tango said after a mile had passed in dry silence. Roberta looked startled, then confused, then angry.

'I don't know what you mean,' she said, 'but if you mean Dane Hollister . . . I might. Except that I know him for a killer: like. . . .'

Tango knew she had nearly said 'Like you are.' But he lowered his hat and stared across the desert flats, not replying. Eventually he had to ask, 'How do you know?'

Roberta shrugged her narrow shoulders beneath her white blouse. 'Father used to have a Texas newspaper mailed to him. A friend sent them from Austin. Mainly he wanted to see how the beef market was doing. For myself, with little else to do around the ranch, I read the paper from beginning to end. In one issue I found a story about Dane Hollister. With the slowness of mail delivery out here, Dane had already been hired on at the ranch by the time I saw the article, and so I recognized the name immediately.

'Dane Hollister murdered a Texas state assemblyman's son down that way – cut his throat with a knife!' She looked to Tango for a reaction. He said:

'Did you ask Dane about it? Things aren't always what they appear to be.'

'No! I did not ask him.'

'Your father must have known something about it. Yet he took Dane on.'

'My father,' she said stiffly, 'was always an easy mark for ne'er-do-wells, drifters and down at the heels bums.'

Tango wondered which group she had fitted him into. He himself had never heard Dane Hollister mention anything about trouble on his backtrail, but it figured in a way. Hollister obviously had a fine education behind him. Now he was riding the desert sands.

'Didn't he ever say anything to you?' Roberta asked, and now Tango thought he saw a gleam of hope in her eyes.

'No. A man doesn't bring his troubles West with him. And if a man's your friend, you don't probe too deeply into his past.'

'I know that,' Roberta said. 'It's just . . . oh, look – I can see Dos Picos.'

SIX

The meeting was held in the office of the banker, Amos Blount. Roberta was calm, yet fidgety. Her dark hair sometimes draped itself loosely over her face and she would brush it aside or blow at it with a puff of breath. She had endured a lot in the last few days.

Tango sat in the corner, hat on his crossed knee. The judge was Malcolm Thomas, a pudgy, slick-jawed, pink-faced man who didn't seem to be thirty years of age yet. Amos Blount sat behind his desk, looking deeply worried. The town marshal of Dos Picos was there – a narrow, somber man called Morgan Teal, who more than once let his eyes rake Tango, uncertain as to who he might be, where he might have seen Tango before.

'There certainly seems to be some impropriety here,' Judge Thomas was saying. 'This Frank Baker, you say, never had authorization from your father to conduct his business affairs?'

'Certainly not,' Roberta said.

'There is no doubt as to this woman's identity?' Thomas asked and the banker and marshal both replied that there certainly was not any doubt as to Roberta Madison's identity.

The judge continued, 'Had your father drawn a will?'

'Yes, but of course I do not have it with me on account of the way I was forced to . . . escape from my own home.'

'The court will need to examine that, in case there is some sort of codicil that assigns management of the Double M ranch to Frank Baker. Such provisions are sometimes entered when there are juvenile heirs, or simply to provide experienced management if there is a doubt that the legatee is capable of assuming the respon- sibilities.' It was hot in Blount's small office, but the judge was the only one noticeably perspiring. He mopped at his smooth pink face with a handkerchief.

'Even if there were such a condition – which I assure you there wasn't,' Roberta said, 'at the time Baker executed the deal for the timber with Gage and Company my father was still very much alive. He had no right to make any such arrangement. If my father hadn't been murdered—'

Now Marshal Teal's head came up. He had been seem- ingly dozing in the heat, but now it was obvious that he had been paying careful attention. 'No one said anything about a murder before.'

'Well, it was murder!' Roberta said too loudly. She leaned back in her chair limply. 'He was poisoned with tea made of jimson weed.'

'Oh?' Judge Thomas blinked as if he were startled. 'Have you experience in pharmacology, Miss Madison? Are you perhaps a physician?'

'No, but according to knowledgeable people. . . .' she stuttered.

The marshal drawled a question: 'Was Frank Baker in the habit of making tea for your father, Miss?'

'I only know,' Roberta said, leaning forward with her

hands between the knees of her divided riding-skirt, 'that this is how it happened.'

'How you suspect it happened,' Judge Thomas corrected her. 'It would be extremely difficult to prove such an allegation without substantial evidence.'

'Frank Baker did it,' Roberta maintained, 'or had it done.'

'Can we return to matters about which we have certain knowledge?' Judge Thomas asked. 'Marshal Teal?'

The lawman turned his steely eyes on Tango, 'You have admitted shooting a logger.'

'He was protecting me!' Roberta insisted, not liking the turn of events. She had come to lodge a complaint, not to defend herself or Tango.

Tango seemed unperturbed. 'I shot him. The man was trespassing, brandishing a rifle.'

'No complaint has been filed against you – yet,' Judge Thomas said. 'Let's get back to what we know and what we can do. Mr Blount, you witnessed Gage and Company making a payment to the purported agent of the Double M ranch?'

'I did,' Amos Blount said. 'An account was opened for Frank Baker; the money deposited.'

'That account will have to be frozen until we get to the bottom of this,' the pink-faced young judge said. 'And to do that, Miss Madison, we will need to see the will your father left. Otherwise. . . .' He spread his hands.

'Otherwise Frank Baker's word is as good as mine!' Roberta asked in a stunned voice.

'The court will need to see the evidence,' Thomas answered stolidly. 'If there is fraud involved, justice will be served.'

'When?' Roberta asked, her voice breaking. This seemed to be the last straw as far as her composure went.

'When all of the facts have been reviewed.'

'After he has stolen our cattle herd and sold it off?' she asked, standing now.

'What cattle herd?' Marshal Teal asked, but he got no answer to his question.

'Miss,' Judge Thomas said in what he supposed was a placatory voice. 'You must see the law's position. A determination of whether Mr Baker had the authority to act on your father's behalf must be based on evidence. As for driving your cattle to sale, is he not the foreman of the Double M?'

'He was . . . is . . . I don't know,' Roberta said poking at her hair nervously. 'What do I have to do? Fire him?'

'You could, but not until after the will is probated. Until then,' Thomas said showing some sensitivity, 'the courts cannot even determine whether the ranch is legally yours. Patience is called for.'

'Patience!' Roberta exploded. There was no telling what else she might have been ready to say. At that moment, Tango who had been quiet for the most part, rose, took her elbow and said:

'Let's find you a hotel room. You need some rest.'

'I've seen my father die! I've seen criminals selling my legacy, and the law . . . the law,' she said, her voice lowering to the hissing menace of a wildcat's, 'has done nothing. Very well, this will be taken care of open-range style.'

Roberta Madison, with her dark hair newly brushed and falling around her shoulders, sat at her hotel room window, watching dusk color the skies and the long desert.

She and Tango had shared a supper in the hotel dining room – if the low-ceilinged, crowded, smoky room could be called that. After eating and resting, Roberta had regained some calmness. Things had not gone well for her that day. The law had not offered much consolation; little support when she needed it most.

Tango had said, 'The law is kind of wrapped up in its self-spun web. If you haven't run up against it before, it can be kind of frustrating. You just have to remember that it's not justice they're primarily interested in, but their legal books.'

'Well,' Roberta had answered unhappily. 'I don't know how that can be. I mean, they know I am my father's daughter, they know that Baker is trying to pull a fast one.'

'They don't know anything until it's been proved in a court of law – meaning the person with the best lawyer is always going to win. Common sense doesn't enter into this. You shouldn't have made that remark about open-range justice,' Tango told her. 'I think they call that threatening mayhem, something like that. They could have arrested you for that alone.'

'Arrested?' Roberta was indignant.

'Yes, Roberta. If I'd said it, I probably would have gotten locked up. I suppose they just took it as the ranting of a hysterical woman.'

Roberta was briefly too angry to speak. She enjoyed little of the rest of her dinner. Back in her room she undressed and sat at the mirror, brushing her hair. She remembered now that her father had said once in a solemn moment when he was having a land dispute, 'The law is always right because it says so.' He had thrown down

71

the papers he had been studying and stamped off out into the yard.

At the time Roberta had not really been listening. She supposed that she had been too young, too self-absorbed to know what Kent Madison had meant. Now she thought she had an inkling.

As Tango had escorted her back toward her room, he paused and told her one more thing that disturbed her deeply. 'Roberta,' he had said quite sincerely, 'you know that they will never find your father's will in that house – not now.'

Much as she found that hard to believe, she supposed it made sense. Baker had taken over her house and, with Rita's help, he would go through the files, the desk until he found that will, struck a match and watched as it burned.

She clenched her fists in anger and frustration. She now had only the Rose Canyon gang to trust and to rely upon. They would fight for her, or so they had all promised. It was comforting, but at the same time she did not want any of them to have to die for her. Not Sparky, shy Toby Leland, Tango. Or Dane Hollister.

She wondered now if she had done Dane an injustice in accepting the fact that he was guilty of a heinous crime without even hearing his side of things. Dane had been guilty in her own mind – yet Dane had never even stood trial. Roberta's world had suddenly become a lot larger and much more confusing than it had been only a few days before.

She wondered where the big-shouldered, studious man was on this night; she gave her hair another few strokes which caused it to crackle, threw the brush down and dropped on to her bed to think of Dane . . . and of Emily Dickinson.

'Only a very lonely woman, indeed!' she said out loud. Then she threw herself over on to her face to try for sleep.

Sparky had held off riding to the Double M until dusk cooled the land. His horse was tired and overheated and so was he. Now he crossed the desert flats as the sky colored, seeing the angles of the house beyond the oak grove. There were lights in some of the windows, but of course no smoke rising from the chimneys in this heat. From far away he could hear the sounds of restless cattle lowing. They had been pushed from their normal range and now were nervously bunched, waiting to be driven to market.

Sparky circled the house, riding directly to the long, low bunkhouse beyond. A scattering of cottonwood trees flanked the building, and there too he saw light showing in several of the high, narrow windows. He patted the note written by Roberta Madison, which he carried in his vest pocket and hoped that there were none of Frank Baker's new-hires sleeping in the bunkhouse. But, with Roberta evicted from her home, there was no reason for those four to leave the comforts of the big house.

He swung down cautiously in the shadows of the cottonwoods at the side of the building and made his way to the front steps of the bunkhouse. He paused and listened; it was silent inside. Sparky stepped up on to the porch and went in. He found Gomez, busy making up his bedroll and he was relieved when the broad-faced, good-natured hand turned toward him with a smile.

'Hey, Sparky, what you doing back?'

73

'I need to talk to you for a minute,' Sparky said, walking across the splintered plank floor to where Gomez waited, blinking questioningly. 'I have a note here from Roberta Madison.' He removed it from his vest pocket. Gomez took it, turned it one way and then the other. He asked:

'What she say?'

Sparky winced, It had not occurred to him that Gomez might not be able to read, No matter: 'Show it to Allison or Sully, they'll tell you.'

'Allison, Sully, Kramer are all out with the herd. We're going to start them with the moonrise this night, to save them from some of the heat. I am only here because I was asleep and have not got my gear ready.'

'Gomez, this is very important. If you are riding out to join the herd, show this letter to someone. Frank Baker is stealing those cattle.'

'Is stealing?' Gomez asked in bewilderment.

'Yes. Remember, this is very important!'

From behind Sparky a deep voice asked, 'What's important, Red?' He turned to fund Hummel watching him, smiling the smile of the vindictive. 'You alone?' he asked, walking slowly across the room, 'or have you brought the famous Drew Tango with you?'

'He's outside,' Sparky lied weakly. The big, bearded man obviously did not believe him. As Gomez inched away Hummel continued forward. Sparky could smell whiskey on the man. This was no barroom, but the encounter was similar, although this meeting promised to have a different outcome.

Now what? Sparky could draw, fire, but that would only summon the others from the main house. Even if he somehow managed to outshoot Hummel, even if he killed

74

him, the others would undoubtedly gun him down. He could attempt that. . . .

Or he could take a beating.

Well, he decided, I can only give it my best. He lifted his fists as the bearish Hummel, spoiling for a fight, came steadily forward.

'You're not supposed to be here, Red,' Hummel said as he bunched his fists.

There was no point in telling Hummel the story he had devised to explain his presence: that he had only come back to the Double M to try to get his old job back. It would not matter to Hummel. Whether he believed the story or not, he meant to beat Sparky. He came onward; Sparky involuntarily backed away. Gomez picked up his bedroll and sidled toward the door. Sparky struck first – he figured he had to. He jabbed twice with all of his strength at Hummel's face, drawing blood from the big man's nose. Instead of discouraging Hummel, it caused something that might have been a smile to crease his face. He came on.

Sparky found himself backed up against one of the bunk beds now. Nowhere to run. He lowered his head and moved in, driving two right-hand shots into Hummel's ribs. The man grunted but did not yield. He slammed a terrific right-hand hook of his own which caught Sparky on the shoulder and knocked him off balance. Sparky managed to duck under another shot from the big man and he stamped down hard on the arch of Hummel's foot with the heel of his boot.

That did it – now Hummel was enraged. He swung wildly with both hands. Frothing at the mouth, cursing in a strangled voice, he caught Sparky first on the skull and then on the point of his chin. There were a dozen more punishing blows, but Sparky felt none of them. He went out on his feet and finally sagged to the floor of the bunkhouse, and past it into a vortex of cold, inky silence.

When Sparky came to he found himself outside under the cottonwood trees. Hummel had apparently dragged him out of the bunkhouse and deposited him there. Sparky could see stars shining beyond the branches of the trees like bright Christmas ornaments. He tried to sit up, and his head exploded with pain. He lay back, trying to keep his stomach from revolting on him. When next he found the inclination to try rising, an hour must have passed. The stars had shifted their position. This time, instead of going directly to his feet, Sparky rolled over on to hands and knees and stayed there like a stunned beast, afraid to move further. Each small motion brought a new surge of pain.

Horse, he thought – he had to find his horse and make it back to Rose Canyon. There was a strange light in the sky, and he could hear the distant lowing of cattle. The bunkhouse and the main house were completely dark. Then he realized that the light in the night sky was the rising moon and, by its glow, the herd was already being moved.

Sparky crawled to the trunk of a cottonwood tree and used it to lever himself up. Panting, head splitting he stood there for a long minute, trying to think, trying to remember where he had left his horse – if they had not found it and taken it away.

By the time he did move, the moon had fully risen and its golden glow painted long shadows beneath the trees and lit the yard faintly. Staggering like a drunk he made his way back toward where he thought he had left his horse tied. The little dun stood there patiently cropping grass. Sparky was never so glad to see an animal in his life.

He approached the horse, leaned his head against its flank and left it there for a long minute before he looked at the saddle and tried to decide whether he could scale its heights. Slowly, painfully, he gathered up his reins and stepped into the stirrup. With sheer determination he managed to swing his leg over and plant his other boot in the stirrup on that side.

Success! Sparky smiled inwardly. He knew now how a convalescent can feel such triumph over his first few steps on the long road back to health.

'Let's go back,' he said to the horse in a slurred voice, and he turned the dun's head, riding the long trail back toward Rose Canyon.

SEVEN

'We have to get after them,' Sparky said, his voice muffled and difficult to understand. He had puffed lips, a swollen jaw and a nearly shut black eye. Hummel had done a thorough job of beating him. Sparky sat on the flat rock, blanket over his shoulders. Dane doubted that he could stand. When Sparky had reached camp he had been slumped in the saddle, holding damaged ribs. Dane had to catch him when he tried to dismount from his dun horse.

'No,' Dane said forcefully. Toby Leland had returned from the springs with a cool, damp cloth for Sparky to place across his damaged face.

'They'll get away,' Sparky said, or at least that sounded like what he was trying to say.

'You need your rest, Sparky,' Dane said, crouching down in front of the redhead, his hand on Sparky's shoulder. 'A cattle herd unused to the trail is a slow moving mass, and they won't try to push them to much speed on a night drive. Besides, we'd better wait until Tango and Roberta get back. This is no time to split our forces. We'll catch up with them,' Dane said, rising again, 'don't worry

78

about that just now.'

Morning returned with a brief, brilliant flourish of color across the eastern sky. Without the early-rising Tango around, the three had slept in longer than usual. Dan awoke, stretched his thick arms and then came fully awake; there were things to be done and they were wasting time. Still, he thought as he rolled his bed up, what was there to do until Tango and Roberta returned? Perhaps, Dane thought as he woke Leland up, they should leave Sparky behind and ride after the herd themselves. But he and Leland against the men traveling with the herd was not enough to stop them. With Tango's gun and Roberta's opportunity to talk to the regular Double M hands, they had a better chance of putting a crimp in Frank Baker's plans.

'Should I rouse Sparky?' Leland asked. His expression was concerned, doleful.

'Let him sleep as long as he can. He took a serious beating. It's a wonder that this Hummel didn't finish the job.' Which was probably, Dane reflected, because the herd was ready to go and his presence was required; certainly it was not left undone out of any sense of mercy. He had never so much as seen Hummel, but he had developed a particular distaste for the man.

The sun rose higher. Leland and Dane Hollister breakfasted on the last of the salt biscuits and spring water. After finishing their poor meal, they visited the spring to refill their canteens. Whatever they decided to do, it was going to be a long hot day. Leland was smiling, an odd expression since Dane saw nothing at all amusing about their situation.

'What's so funny, Toby?'

'Us. Right over there is a working cattle ranch with thousands of pounds of beef roaming around and we're going hungry.'

Dane saw the irony and he nodded. With all that had been going on they had not so much as shot a deer. Shots in the canyon would have echoed down as far as the flats. Dane did not think that Frank Baker had any idea that they were holed up there. Now it seemed not to matter. That very morning he had seen a four-point buck come down from the high reaches to dip its muzzle in the cool water of the spring, but he had not taken a shot. They did not know for certain how many of the hired guns had taken the trail with the herd and how many might have been left to guard the home ranch.

It was another two hours with the sun already riding high when they heard the clatter of hoofs over the rocky floor of the canyon below them. Dane automatically snatched up his Henry repeater and stepped away from the camp to partially conceal himself behind a massive gray boulder, but it was only Tango and Roberta returning and he stepped out to greet the two desert-weary riders.

'Welcome home!' Dane said with forced cheerfulness, but he got no smiles in return. Tango looked solemn; Roberta was flushed with the heat. Her straw hat shaded her face, but did nothing to cool her. Tango swung down from his sorrel horse wearily and took the reins to Roberta's little gray as she slipped stiffly from the saddle. Her expression was no brighter than Tango's and Dane knew from their grim expressions that they had accomplished little in Dos Picos.

'I'll water the ponies,' Tango volunteered, leading the animals toward the spring. He obviously did not want to talk.

Dane led Roberta to the flat rock, the surface of which was already hot, spread his striped horse blanket for the woman to sit on and tilted back his hat, waiting. After some moments he had to prompt her:

'Well? How did it go?'

'They are not even sure that I own the Double M,' Roberta had to tell him, turning her eyes on Dane. Those shining eyes seemed older than just the day before.

'How can they. . . ?'

'They say there has to be a will so the court can determine my father's intent. And, since Frank Baker is the foreman of the Double M, he had the right to begin a planned cattle drive to market.'

Dane was furious, but he answered calmly enough, 'We can't let Baker do that. If he reaches Tucson and finds out that the timber deal has fallen through, he'll out his losses, take what he can get for the steers and vanish.'

'If we could find the will . . . but it wouldn't be in time, would it?' Roberta asked.

'No. The law moves too slowly. We'll have to take care of matters ourselves. Besides, I don't think it's safe for you to return to the house just now. We don't know who's there or what they might try '

'But. . . .' Roberta began, but at that moment she heard a pained groan and saw Sparky struggling to sit up in bed, His face was shades of purple, red and yellow. She had heard fighting men call it a sundown face, but she had never understood the term until now. 'My God, Sparky! What happened to you?'

Dane answered for him. 'He tried to take your note to the ranch hands and got found out by the man, Hummel.'

'I'm so sorry, Sparky,' Roberta said as Sparky managed

to sit, arms wrapped loosely around his sprawled knees. Something that might have been intended as a smile lifted one corner of his battered mouth. 'Then, Dane, does this mean that the other men – Gomez, Kramer, Allison and Sully have no idea that they're driving a stolen herd south?'

'That's what it means.'

'And so far as we know the loggers have returned to Mammoth Point by now with more guns and probably legal protection. I'm doomed,' Roberta said disconsolately. She dropped her face to hide it against drawn-up knees.

'We'll clean this all up,' promised Toby Leland, who had arrived to watch the young woman, her narrow shoulders shuddering beneath the fabric of her white blouse. Dane had never seen Leland look so determined before. His boyish face was set with purpose. Tango was back, leading the refreshed horses into camp. He looked the small gathering over and let his focus settle on the badly bruised Sparky.

'Hummel?'

'Yes,' Sparky managed to lisp.

Tango nodded, took one of his canteens from his saddle horn and tossed it to Sparky. 'Better keep on drinking as much water as you can tolerate. It'll be a long ride.'

'He can't. . . .' Roberta said, lifting her face.

'Yes I can!' Sparky shouted. The explosion of breath brought racking pain to a damaged rib and he clutched his side. 'You think I'm going to let them get away with what they're trying to do to you, Roberta?' He paused, drank and said with his eyes flashing, 'You think I'm going to let Hummel get away with what he did to me?'

'We don't have any food,' Leland said pragmatically. 'Maybe we should try going to the big house for supplies. After all, Carlos is bound to be there even if Cooky is driving the chuck wagon for the trail herd.'

'Carlos will be there,' Dane said, 'but what about Rita? And who else? We don't know if Baker is with the herd. Or Jeb Fry.'

'Oh,' Leland said blankly.

'Tighten your belt another notch,' Sparky recommended, 'We have to track down those cattle thieves before they reach market.'

'You, Sparky,' Roberta said with apprehension, 'surely you should remain behind.'

'I'd be just as hungry here,' Sparky said, rising with extreme effort. 'And only half as safe.'

'Saddle up, men,' Tango said. 'We're riding.'

Tango and Dane agreed that the cattle herd would be moved south along the Little Legend Creek. The stock would need water, and that was the way they had always been driven in the past. The Rose Canyon gang didn't have to concern itself with following the winding stream. Their canteens were full and they could cut a straight course to head off the herd. Even though the cattle had a full night's start on them, they would have to be halted somewhere along the way to drink and to rest, if Baker or whoever was driving the herd didn't want to see one steer after another dropping off on the trail simply because they could not go on.

The going wasn't bad. The land was mostly gray sand and patches of red pumice stone dotted with scattered creosote bushes and mesquite trees, with the occasional saguaro cactus here and there looking like surprised matrons, hands uplifted. Along the dry wash bottoms gray willow brush stood in thick clumps, looking for all the world like dead vegetation. They would look like that until it rained and water rushing down from the peaks brought them to flourishing life along what would briefly be rushing creeks. It was the desert way; all of these plants had a way of hiding their life force, their blooms for months until sudden moisture brought green newness and color to the sere vegetation.

Roberta rode close beside Dane now. They kept their eyes on Sparky, who was only staying in the saddle through sheer grit. Leland's face was set, lacking the fearfulness he had earlier displayed although their situation was more dire than it had ever been. Tango, on his long-legged sorrel with the white blaze and a white stocking on one rear leg, rode a little away from them, his expression hidden by the shadow of his wide-brimmed black Stetson hat.

'Will we catch up with them?' Roberta asked. 'In time, I mean?'

'You can't sell a herd of cattle in half a day no matter how eager the beef buyers might be. We have time.'

'I don't see what we can do to stop it if the buyers in Tucson are also convinced that Frank Baker has the right to sell the cattle.'

Dane grinned, 'We go to the law again. If they can't stop Baker, they can delay him quite a while.'

'And if we lose. . . ?'

'I don't intend to let it get that far,' Dane answered. 'We'll cut them off long before they reach Tucson.'

'And then?' Roberta asked.

'You speak to the Double M hands, tell them what is

84

happening. We'll turn the herd around and take it home. You know they'll listen to you.'

'Yes, yes, I know they will,' Roberta said, still doubtful as she guided her gray horse around a nasty-looking clump of barrel cactus. 'But Dane,' she said with fear in her eyes. 'Frank Baker and his men, they won't give up the herd willingly.'

'No.'

'And men will be killed, won't they?'

'It seems,' Dane answered, 'a distinct possibility.'

'All for me! It doesn't seem fair.'

'It's not all for you,' Dane corrected. 'It's for Kent Madison, who gave all of us a break at one time or another. These men ride for the brand, Roberta. No one is allowed to steal from the Double M. It's the same as stealing from each man personally. I don't know what Allison and Gomez will do, but I think I know them and Kramer and Sully well enough to know they'll fight with us once they understand the truth of things. If they don't, well, they can just ride away. The four of us, the Rose Canyon gang, we will fight, and that's that.'

'But you might be shot down!'

'Look around, look at the men's faces. I think it's gone beyond us caring for our own lives, Roberta. It is a matter of honor, and you know what that means to a Western man.'

'I'm only just beginning to understand it,' she said. Dane glanced at her, watched her long dark hair weave and dance in the breeze. He smiled.

'Dane?' Roberta asked after another half-mile during which they crested a low quartz gravel-strewn knoll, and could see, far away, the green line of vegetation that marked the course of the meandering Little Legend Creek.

'Yes?'

'Tell me about it. I want to know. Tell me about the man you killed in Austin.'

'Did your father tell you that?'

'No. I just found out,' Roberta answered. 'Please tell me, Dane. It's important to me.'

Dane took a deep, slow breath and kept his eyes on the eastern skies. He did not want to tell the story, but Roberta was insistent and seemed utterly sincere in her need to understand, so Dane told her.

'I was still a medical student and I was invited to a dinner party at the state capitol – mainly because I was courting a girl who was related to one of the governor's aides. All the men wore their best suits, the women their fanciest dresses. I felt that I was going to achieve great things, being introduced to all sorts of influential people.

'There was supposed to be a speech after dinner. I can't even remember who was giving it, what it was supposed to be about. I was seated with . . . my girlfriend, next to a state assemblyman's son. He was a bright good-looking young man. Very personable. I had been talking to him when he started choking. His face went utterly white and then bluish. He was epileptic, it seems, and he was having a seizure. In fact he had swallowed his tongue and was unable to breathe. He toppled out of his chair as women screamed and men moved away.

'There is a medical process called a tracheotomy – do you know what that is?'

'No,' Roberta admitted.

'It's becoming more common now, but it wasn't well

known then. It involves cutting an artificial breathing hole in the windpipe of a strangling victim so that he can draw air into his lungs when the normal passage is blocked,' Dane explained.

'I had never seen it attempted before, certainly not done it, but the boy was writhing on the floor, dying before my eyes. No one else was making a move. But, as I say, I was a medical student and thought that I had to attempt the procedure or watch him die. With a knife from the table I attempted to make an incision, but he was thrashing around. My knife missed its mark and I ended up severing his carotid artery.

'I stood trembling, watching as the sudden rush of blood spread across the ballroom floor. The eyes around me . . . no one understood what I had been trying to do. They just saw me take a knife to the young man's throat And kill him.'

'But, Dane. . . .'

'That's enough! That's the end. That was the end of my medical career, the end of my romance, the end of any ambitions I ever had. No more, please!' he said, his voice growing bitter.

Roberta nodded and continued on in silence through the heat of day. She had learned what she wished to know; but her curiosity had brought a flood of bad memories back to Dane Hollister. She felt ashamed of herself for causing the big-shouldered, gentle man pain.

As she watched, Tango crested another small gray knoll where scattered yucca grew. He held up his hand as he squinted into the distance, studying the scene. As they approached him he glanced around, then jabbed a finger toward the line of the watercourse with flourishing green plants lining its banks. And there! a dark collection of animals stood, tiny as ants at this distance. It was the herd. They had caught up. Tango muttered:

'This is it, boys, check your loads.'

They trailed down toward the river. The cattle were strung out along the lazily flowing stream, drinking. Dane caught a glimpse of the canvas of Cooky's chuck wagon through the trees. Tango halted his horse again in the shade of three closely bunched sycamores and said:

'You'd better wait here, Sparky.'

'I will not,' Sparky answered indignantly. 'I've got someone to settle matters with.'

'And you're in no shape to do it,' Tango replied. 'Not only would you be of no help, we'll have to spend half of our time worrying about you.'

'All right,' Sparky conceded. He had to admit that he was in no shape for a fight. 'Someone help me down and I'll wait here for the rest of you.'

They left Sparky propped up against the trunk of a sycamore and walked their horses forward. The horses, scenting water now, tugged eagerly at the reins. 'How do you want to do this, Tango?' Dane asked.

'First thing is to tell the Double M hands what's happening. With all of them on our side, it might not even come down to fighting. Baker's men wouldn't have a chance.'

As if on cue Mike Sully appeared, weaving his way through the trees. His handlebar mustache, his pride and joy, was sagging badly, the wax he used to shape it melted. In astonishment he pulled up, his eyes searching them and resting at last on Roberta Madison.

'Why, Miss Madison. What are you doing way out here?'

'I've come to take my herd back,' she said coolly. In response to Sully's stunned expression, she explained. 'Father has died, and Frank Baker is trying to sell off everything that belongs to the Double M. Where is he, by the way?'

'Frank isn't with us,' Sully told them. 'He stayed back on the ranch with that Jeb Fry fellow. He said he had some other important business to take care of.'

'The lumber,' Dane said.

'What?' Sully asked in confusion.

'We'll tell you later,' Roberta said. 'For now you have to get the word to the other boys. This herd is turning for home range.'

Sully touched his mustache, frowning. Then he said, 'You're the boss, Miss Madison, But what do I tell those two yahoos that Frank Baker sent along on this drive?'

'His hired guns?'

'I guess that's what they are,' Sully answered, 'They're sure not cowhands.'

'We'll tell them,' Tango said. There was steel in his voice. 'Just tell Gomez, Allison and Kramer to meet us over here so we can explain.'

'All right,' Sully said with a shrug of resignation.

'Wait,' Dane Hollister said. 'You say there are only two of Baker's men making the drive?'

'That's right. One of them's named Hummel, the other Sturgis.'

'That leaves us with one man unaccounted for,' Dane told Tango. He didn't like that. In a battle unknowns could be deadly.

'Get the hands gathered, Sully,' Tango said. 'If Hummel or Sturgis sees you and asks what's going on, use any sort

89

of lie to divert them.'

As they watched Mike Sully making his way back to the river, Dane commented. 'It's better than I thought. We're seven against their two now.'

Tango noticed that Dane had not included Sparky in his count. Leland sat his horse in silence. There seemed to be relief in his eyes. He had not relished the idea of going up against five rough men with their small crew.

They waited, their horses shifting their feet in the spirit of the overhanging trees, and in half an hour Sully was back. Behind him rode Gomez, Allison and Kramer. Briefly Roberta told the Double M hands what had happened. There seemed to be no doubt on their faces. Dane thought that if he, Tango and Toby Leland had arrived alone these men might have had some reservations about fighting for these three cast-offs. With Roberta there to tell the tale, the hands took everything as a matter of fact. Roberta was a much-loved woman and she alone held the rights to the Double M ranch and its possessions. She had Kent Madison's authority behind her and none of them would ever have thought of disobeying Madison.

'What now, Tango?' asked Jake Allison, a lanky, hard-faced man out of Arkansas.

'If we ride to face them in a bunch we probably won't have to go to shooting. They'll see that we have the numbers, maybe figure that Frank Baker has overplayed his hand, and ride on their way.'

'That's the way,' agreed Hal Kramer, who removed his battered hat to mop at his bald head with his red scarf. 'I saw Sturgis just now at the rear of the chuck wagon, talking to Cooky. The other one – Hummel, I don't know where he is.'

90

'We'll deal with that one first,' Dane said. 'Suggest that he heel his pony out of the area. Hummel will show up eventually. We'll handle him then.'

'They won't be happy,' Tango commented. 'Baker promised them a big payday.'

'Tough,' Dane said. 'They ought to chalk this up to experience and thank their lucky stars that we're letting them ride off in one piece.'

'We take his guns, eh?' Gomez asked. But Tango shook his head.

'That would make the man angrier than anything. He's got to earn his living with them – just so he doesn't try it around here.'

In a bunch then, they started toward the day camp. Dane glanced at Roberta and said, 'Just for my peace of mind, will you stay back a little way. I think this will work, but you never know about men with guns.'

They found Sturgis at the rear of the chuck wagon, about to step into leather. His bearish, bearded face came round in surprise, and then anger settled in his features as he spotted Roberta Madison among the riders. Cooky peered around the corner of the wagon; his craggy face twisted into a confused frown, then he quickly disappeared.

'What is this?' Sturgis demanded. He stepped back out of his stirrup and swept back one corner of his jacket to reveal his Colt.

'An uprising,' Dane Hollister said. 'We're taking the herd and you've been voted out of the game.'

'Rustlers!' Sturgis said, wanting to laugh but too angry to do so.

'How can you use that word?' Roberta shouted. 'These

91

are my cattle, not Frank Baker's – certainly they're not yours.'

Sturgis's face grew hotter. Tango had separated himself from the bunch of ranch hands and rode nearer to Sturgis. 'Drew Tango – are you behind this!' Sturgis roared.

'No, But I'm with them. I'm giving you the opportunity to ride, Sturgis. Unless you feel like trying to draw down on seven armed men.'

Sturgis looked as if that wild thought had actually crossed his mind, but he was alone and knew he would find little satisfaction in picking off a few of them only to end his career and life lying dead in the sands along Little Legend.

'Where's Hummel?' Dane asked.

'I don't know,' Sturgis growled. He kept his eyes fixed on Tango, knowing his reputation.

'It doesn't matter; we'll find him,' Tango said. 'For now, straddle that pony of yours and line it out to the south. Don't stop riding until you can't see us, and we can't see you. And don't,' he added menacingly, 'even think about circling back. The game's over. Go find some easier pickings.'

Sturgis wanted to curse Tango, to challenge him, to threaten him, but there was no point in any of it. Sturgis was not a brilliant man, but he was wise enough to know when he was beaten. He decided instead to swing aboard his pinto pony and turn it away from them, venting his fury now with wild curses hurled at Frank Baker.

Hummel circled the camp slowly, moving through the sycamore trees, the dry desert breeze rattling their leaves. What was going on? He had been downriver and returned to find all of the hands grouped together around the chuck wagon, but there were more than four of them. He didn't get a good look as he ducked and silently rode his horse away at a walk, its hoofs making little sound on the sandy soil,

He decided to circle to the west and north and then come up on the gathered men to try to get an idea of what was happening. Sturgis could take care of himself for the time being – there had been no shots fired.

The day remained hot although the river was a cooling influence. Cicadas sang and crows cawed in the treetops. Hummel had to duck low for a low hanging branch, which he pushed aside, then he entered a small clearing where a man sat alone, slumped against a tree in the heated shade.

'Well, well,' Hummel said with dark pleasure. The red-headed man just would not take a hint. Hummel slipped from the saddle and walked softly forward to where Bill Sparks rested.

Sparky was awakened by some unnatural sound or by a deeper instinct to find Hummel, a broken-toothed grin on his bearded face, hunkered over him with his meaty fists bunched.

'If it isn't my favorite target,' Hummel said with savage menace.

EIGHT

Tango had ridden away to the south, following Sturgis along the trail a way just to make sure the man had no intention of turning back. Roberta had kept the men together for a while asking Gomez and the others how long a drive was enough for the cattle on that day. Leland had found the chuck wagon and he was determined to have the best meal Cooky could whip up at short notice. No one could blame the young man.

Dane Hollister decided that the best thing that could be done for the badly beaten Sparky was to have Cooky make up a bed for him in the back of his wagon, and he now returned to the grove where they had left the redhead to tell him what had happened and that he was through with riding for a while.

Moving through the shadows of the trees he came upon Sparky, now standing unsteadily, being half held up by a black-bearded man. Dane swung down from his buckskin and walked that way, Sparky's eyes opened wide as he watched Dane's approach over the big man's shoulder. Seeing the look, Hummel released Sparky and spun.

'Is that the way you got your reputation as a fighter –

beating up on battered men?' Dane asked.

'This one, I'll beat him up again wherever, whenever I find him,' Hummel said in a gravelly voice. 'It's none of your business, cowpoke. Suppose you just get out of here before I invite you to the party as well.'

'Oh, I've already invited myself,' Dane said, unbuckling his gunbelt which he hung over the pommel of his saddle; Hummel frowned at the dark-haired man, noticing the bulging at the shoulders of his shirt. He was big all right, but size meant nothing to Hummel when he was in a fighting mood. Big or small, he fought them all. Sparky eased aside, keeping his hands on the tree for support. Dane Hollister didn't wait for Hummel to come to him, but walked forward, grim determination on his face.

'Good,' Hummel said. 'I've been needing a little exercise. I didn't figure to get much with this sprout.' He removed his own sidearm, more for convenience than out of a sense of fair play. The bearded man stood waiting for Dane to make the first move.

Dane stepped in and winged a right-hand shot at Hummel, but the bearded man blocked it easily with his elbow. Grinning now, Hummel shot two rapid left hooks at Dane, who caught one of the blows on the top of his skull and barely managed to slip the second one. Hummel continued with mechanical precision. Another left and then two stabbing rights were aimed at Dane Hollister. One of these got through Dane's guard and split his lips, starting the blood to flow.

'Well, cowboy!' Hummel bellowed. 'What do you think now?'

Dane didn't respond. He wiped the blood away from his mouth as he circled Hummel, looking for an opening.

95

Dane feinted with his left and then brought an overhand right down on Hummel's ear. It did nothing to stagger him. The big bearded man, his grin now vanished, crowded Dane closer.

Driving Dane up against a tree Hummel began a barrage of body shots that drove the wind out of Dane's lungs. Dane ducked, saw one of Hummel's wild blows strike the tree trunk and came up inside, firing lefts and rights to belly, throat, face. Hummel backed off a little, now appearing slightly puzzled. The cowboy should have gone down by now. They usually did when Hummel landed a few good ones.

Hummel backed away a little to get his own breath back, but now Dane was the aggressor. He moved directly toward Hummel, smashing a lead right into the big man's face. He fired it again and caught Hummel on the neck. For an instant the thug seemed to sway on his feet a little, but he was steady enough to fire two right hooks at Dane. One down low to the ribs, the second catching Dane flush on the jaw.

It was Dane who had to back away this time, clearing his head, where brightly colored cobwebs seemed to want to take up residence. Hummel was all over him, throwing wild punches from each side, from all positions, and Dane felt a tooth crack, felt fresh blood drip from his nose. This was no good, he realized. If he continued boxing the man, Hummel would eventually wear him down. Dane lowered his head, wrapped his arms around Hummel and ran him backwards. Surprised, Hummel had trouble keeping his balance. His back suddenly slammed up against Dane Hollister's buckskin horse and, as the frightened animal sidestepped away, Hummel went down. Dane stepped back. Hummel rose heavily, wiping sweat and blood from his eyes.

'That's all I'm going to take from you, cowboy,' Hummel said from deep in his throat, and like a bear he charged Dane again. Sledge-hammer fists rained down on Dane's shoulders, skull and ribs. All of them were painful, a few stunning, but none of them now jolted him with the power of Hummel's earlier blows. Dane wondered whether Hummel wasn't simply tiring. Dane's boots came up against a fallen log and he toppled over it, slamming the breath from himself as he met the ground hard. Hummel leaped the log and hovered over him, his fists clenched, shirt torn, eyes wild.

Hummel turned vicious. He took it into his head to stomp Dane, to break ribs and skull. It was no longer a simple fistfight; he meant to kill Dane. The bearded man leaped into the air, aiming the heels of his boots at Dane's head. Dane barely managed to roll aside. Scrambling to his feet he found Hummel waiting for him. Crouched and ready, Hummel moved in with intent to destroy Dane Hollister. His chest heaved, both of his eyes were swollen, blood dripped from his right ear.

It came to Dane suddenly: Hummel was beaten, He was continuing out of pride, fighting on reflex alone. Dane got to his toes slightly and jabbed at Hummel's nose. Blood instantly spurted from it. Hummel hadn't his earlier quick strength. He could not find a way to block Dane's punches.

Hummel took another blow to the nose, one to his left eye, one on the hinge of his jaw that sent him staggering to one side, almost falling down. In a low crouch Hummel continued to fight back, his arms held very low, his punches without power. Dane continued to pepper him with left jabs and pinpointed an occasional right-hand shot on the big man's jaw. Hummel staggered again, but he would not go down.

He was little more than a punching bag for Dane now, however, and Dane cut loose with everything he had, lefts, rights, uppercuts, driving the bearded man back. Now Hummel did go down. To one knee only, but his head hung heavily and his fists were half-open as if he no longer had the strength to clench them. He was a beaten man.

'That's enough, Dane!' Tango called. He sat his sorrel horse at the edge of the clearing. 'He's had enough.'

Dane nodded and turned heavily away, feeling stiffness or aching in every muscle of his body. He walked to his horse, hoping no one saw how unsteady he was on his feet. He removed his canteen and splashed water across his face and chest. Wiping the blood from him as best he could, he glanced at Tango and then at Hummel, who remained kneeling, seeming not to possess the strength to rise.

Dane looked at Tango and said, 'It probably would have been easier on both of us just to plug him.'

A bruised and bloody Hummel was warned off in no uncertain terms and he trailed out to the south, body sagged low over his horse's neck. Sparky was taken to the chuck wagon where Cooky had made a rough bed of blankets for him. They helped Sparky up into the wagon, where he half-collapsed on to the pile of blankets.

'Thanks, Dane,' Sparky said. 'Though I think I could have taken him myself.'

Dane went to the river and soaked his battered hands in its cold current. The herd had already been started homeward, Gomez, Allison, Kramer and Sully now doing the job they knew best. There was no sign of Roberta, and Dane asked Tango where she was.

'Riding point with Gomez. She looked around kind of sadly and then heeled her pony out of here,' Tango said. 'What is it with you two? You seem to like each other well enough, but. . . .'

'Shut up, Tango,' Dane said wearily. 'How would I know what the trouble is! She's a woman, isn't she?'

Then he swung heavily into the saddle on his buckskin's back and started northward after the herd. Tango stood there for a moment, grinning. Cooky had come up behind him, having finished harnessing his team of horses. The gnarled little man asked Tango:

'What is it, Drew? Are we going to have a wedding soon?'

'It's got all the signs, Cooky.'

The sun was canting over to the west, casting long shadows. The east face of Mammoth Point was dark with shade as they returned to the Double M. The drovers spread the cattle out across the long grass of their familiar home ground and left them to graze in peace. Then, after making their own arrangements as to night-herding shifts, Gomez and Mike Sully returned first to the bunkhouse, lugging their saddles.

The chuck wagon had rolled in last and now was halted before the bunkhouse, where Tango, Roberta and Dane sat on the porch, enjoying the chance to swing from the saddle. No one had approached the house yet. No one was eager to do so.

'It's quiet,' Roberta said, looking through the oak trees toward the house – her house. 'But we don't know who's in there.'

99

'Anyone would have heard the cattle coming in,' Dane said. 'We have to assume they were waiting to see who came in with them.'

Tango said, 'They could be barricaded in there, gone, or waiting to see how many of their gang was out here. If there is anyone there, it's only Baker and Jeb Fry we have to worry about.'

'There's another man, We don't know his name, but he is unaccounted for,' Dane reminded them.

'Want to buck them?' Tango asked.

'Let's give it a little longer.' Dane Hollister glanced skyward. 'We've got at least two hours of light left.'

'The men,' Roberta said in a lower voice after Sully and Gomez had tramped past them and into the bunkhouse, tipping their hats to her, 'I don't think we can ask them to get any more involved in this.'

'I agree,' Dane said. 'They're just cowboys doing a job as best they can. Unless things get desperate, we ought to leave them out of this.'

'We started the job,' Tango said grimly. 'We'll finish it.'

Eventually Cooky returned to the bunkhouse after freeing his trail horses of their harness. Behind him came Sparky, most of his weight draped across Leland's shoulders. 'Going to cook tonight?' Leland called to the cook.

'I've got to empty out the wagon and put all those stores away,' Cooky said in a grumpy voice. 'First I mean to take a rest on my own bunk. Poor as it might be, it beats sleeping on solid ground.'

Tango rose to assist Toby Leland in bringing Sparky up the steps and into the bunkhouse. 'You can't be hungry all the time,' Tango commented to Leland.

'He has been since the day I met him,' Sparky grunted

as they guided him to an empty lower bunk, rolled out the mattress and placed him on it. 'I'm not much of a help, am I?'

'A man can only do what he can,' Tango said. 'Get some rest.'

'I'm pretty tired of resting,' Sparky said bitterly, but his eyes were already closing.

'I'll call you if we need you,' Tango said and returned to the front porch where Dane and Roberta sat side by side, unspeaking. 'There's someone out there in the oaks,' Tango said, not looking directly that way.

Dane looked startled, then abashed. He had noticed no movement in the trees. 'Come on out, whoever you are,' Dane called as Tango stood to one side, his hand resting near his Colt revolver. It took a few seconds but eventually the small figure appeared. He came forward uncertainly, warily. It was Carlos Real.

The houseman's voice was unsteady as he approached and explained, 'I did not know what was happening. I could not tell who was here.'

'None of Baker's men is here,' Dane told Carlos.

'No?' Carlos said in surprise, but he didn't ask any of the obvious questions.

'Who is at the house, Carlos?' Roberta asked.

'No one – well, only me and Rita,' he answered.

'Baker is gone?'

'Yes. He and the man with the scar – Jeb Fry – they rode out this morning. I heard them say something about Mammoth Point.'

'They must be expecting the loggers to come back,' Dane said. 'Baker would want to make sure. Gage and Company's money will mean a lot to him. He would only

101

have received the first installment after signing the agreement with Gage. The rest depends, I'm sure, on how much timber the loggers take out of there.'

'What about my father?' Roberta asked hesitantly. Carlos removed his hat and held it before him in both hands.

'We had to bury him this morning, Miss Roberta. You understand. There was no ceremony, but it needed to be done.'

'And only Rita is in the house now?' Tango asked.

'Yes. She and myself . . . but I do not think I will stay much longer. Things have become very bad around here.'

'Give it a few more days,' Dane urged. 'Stay in the bunkhouse with the crew if you want.'

'You should have seen them!' Carlos said with excited remembrance. 'My sister and this Frank Baker. They were tearing everything apart. Everything! Even before we had taken Mr Madison away.'

'Looking for the will,' Dane commented. 'Did they find it, Carlos?'

The houseman shrugged. 'I didn't see. I don't know. I was so ashamed of my sister, ashamed for my family. Now Rita has the idea that Frank Baker loves her and that he will make her rich.' Carlos made a disgusted sound. 'It is very bad.'

Roberta got to her feet. 'I think I'll have a talk with Rita,' she said with dark determination.

'I'll go with you,' Dane said, rising. He glanced at Tango. 'Want to come along, Drew?'

'I think the two of you can probably handle her,' Tango said drily. 'I haven't gotten a lot of rest lately. I figure that if I'm going to ride out to Mammoth Point in the

102

morning, I'd better catch some sleep.'

'Is that what you plan to do?' Dane asked.

'I'd better. If Jeb Fry is up there.' Tango did not add anything to his statement, but Dane knew what Tango meant. If the gunfighter Jeb Fry was there, Tango was the only one among them who would stand a chance against him. Even if Dane Hollister's hands were not bruised and swollen as they were, his own chances would be about as great as a midget sent to duel with an elephant.

'Let's go, Dane. If you're coming,' Roberta said a little snappishly. Dane glanced at Tango who was grinning.

It was true, she was already beginning to act like a wife.

Tango watched them walk toward the house through the shadows of the oak trees. Then he went to see to his sorrel before he rolled up in one of the bunkhouse beds for a long night's rest. His last night? Tango frowned as he led his sorrel toward the stable. Maybe. Just maybe, if Jeb Fry was as good as his reputation. With a touch of dark nostalgia Tango reflected on his life and figured, well, there wouldn't be anyone who would miss him much anyway.

There was no caution in Roberta Madison as she stormed into the kitchen at the back of the house. That she was in a fury was obvious to Dane Hollister. There was a little dark woman in the house who had murdered her father, probably at the instigation of Frank Baker. But Rita had done the killing, administering poisoned tea as if she were a loving member of the family. And Roberta had been taken in by her.

Fool that she was, she had let her father slowly die out of misplaced trust. Now they had torn the house apart, trying to make sure that any will Kent Madison had made was destroyed. After that they had simply placed her father in a hastily dug grave, as if he were of no more importance than a dog.

'Rita!' Roberta shouted from the kitchen. She stalked forward into the living room, Dane on her heels. He moved cautiously now, hoping that Carlos's information was correct, but concerned that one of Baker's cohorts could still be in the house, or that Frank Baker himself might have unexpectedly returned.

'Rita!' Roberta screamed again, and Dane saw that her small fists were bunched.

No one answered, but as they crossed the room, they heard a scuttling sound in one of the closets along the right-hand wall. Some small object tinkled to the floor. Roberta started that way determinedly, Dane wanted to urge caution, but he knew he could not hold her back. Roberta rattled the handle on the closet. It seemed someone inside was holding it shut, but then she braced herself and with both hands flung the door open to discover Rita cowering within.

Her eyes were wide, white in her dark face. 'Miss. . . .' Then she gave up any idea of talking herself out of trouble. The anger on Roberta's face was too obvious. Quicker than seemed possible the woman ducked under Roberta's arm and hoisted her skirts, darting toward the stairs leading to the second story.

If Rita had seemed quicker than a mouse, Roberta, energized, seemed quicker than a cat. Rita reached the third step on the staircase before Roberta lunged and caught the escaping maid by the ankle. Rita hit the stairs with a thud of flesh and bone against solid wood and she shrieked once, trying to turn to fight off Roberta.

Roberta simply continued to grip Rita's ankle, dragging her back down the steps by her boot.

'You treacherous little beast!' Roberta said. Now Rita, whimpering, was on her back and Roberta was sitting on her, her face furious.

'I didn't do nothing,' Rita sobbed, but Roberta was having none of it.

'Nothing but murder my father! I ought to kill you!' Roberta screamed.

'Roberta,' Dane cautioned in a soft voice. 'Let's not make a bad thing worse.'

'No,' Roberta panted, sitting back, running her fingers through her wildly disarranged dark hair. 'Where is my father's will, Rita? I know you have it. It wouldn't have been too hard for you to find after working for my father for six years.'

'I don't know,' Rita said, cringing. She looked as if she thought Roberta might start raining blows on her. Dane wasn't so sure himself.

'You'd better leave, Dane,' Roberta said. 'Or at least turn your back, because I am going to search this little liar down to her petticoats.'

'Try her boots first,' Dane said calmly. For he had seen a suspicious fragment of yellow above the top of Rita's left boot.

'No!' Rita screamed, but before she could do much else, Roberta was gripping both of her feet and Dane had slipped off her boot.

Inside was the last will and testament of Kent Madison.

'Little thief,' Roberta panted, rising. 'Little murderer.'

Rita said nothing. She curled up on the floor and lay

there whimpering. Dane, who had briefly studied the document, now handed it to Roberta. 'We'll go over it later,' Dane said.

'I wonder why Baker trusted her with the will?' Roberta said.

'I doubt he did. I think that Rita found it and never told Frank Baker that she had,' Dane said, studying the pathetic creature at their feet.

'But why?'

'Frank Baker had promised her a lot. Wealth, maybe even marriage. But what if Frank's scheming came to grief? As it will. Then what would become of Rita? Your father was a kind and generous man. Carlos and Rita would have been provided for in his will. Not enough to make her wealthy, but enough to support herself on.'

'Yes,' Roberta agreed. 'I know there will be some such bequest in the will. Just to repay Rita for her many years of faithful service.'

The anger was gone from Roberta now, transformed into deep, inconsolable grief. She went to Dane, her father's will clenched tightly in one hand. She put her arms around him, leaned her forehead against his chest, and began trembling as the tears began to flow.

They both looked around at the sounds of movement, to find Rita on her knees, hands uplifted. 'What will you do to me? They will hang me or Frank Baker will kill me for what I have done.'

'Just go,' Roberta answered spacing out her words. 'Take a horse, take a buggy, take your kitchen utensils, whatever you want. Just go! Go far away and try hiding your shame. I don't want ever to see your face again. You have half an hour. If you're still here after that, you'll be

106

hogtied and delivered to Marshal Teal in Dos Picos.'

Rita rose, fearful, yet nursing some hope of deliver-ance. In the back of her cunning little mind she must have thought that she had outsmarted the world again, Dane watched her with sullen eyes. As she turned to retreat, he asked her:

'Rita? What really killed Calvin McGraw?'

NINE

'Miss Madison, she say half an hour or I see the marshal,' a fearful Rita Real said after they had placed her on one of the brown leather sofas to face Dane and Roberta. She sat, hands clasped between her knees.

'The half-hour will start after you answer my question,' Dane replied.

'It was, I think,' Rita replied with a heavy sigh, 'about two years ago Frank Baker came to me and what he said was something like: "You are too pretty a girl to be doing the kind of work you are doing." He took my hands and turned them over in his. They were very red after washing up the morning dishes, And I knew as he stood near me . . . I thought I knew, that he was the man I had been waiting for. He told me that one day he meant to own the Double M Ranch.

Rita poked nervously at her dark, lank hair. 'I kissed him. He made me many promises, and I believed them all. After a while he asked me to make a special tea for Mr McGraw to have with his lunch.' She hesitated, started to lie, then said, 'I knew what the leaves he gave me were. I know jimson weed, but I did what Frank told me, I put a

108

lot of sugar in the tea to mask the strong taste of it. Mr McGraw, he seemed hardly to notice. He was not particular about what he ate or drank. His mind was always on something else, on ranch business.'

'It started that long ago!' Roberta exclaimed. 'Rita, didn't you know that you were dabbling in murder?'

Rita's eyes were filled with insincere grief. 'Frank, he told me that he hated McGraw. He said that McGraw was going to fire him because he thought that Frank was stealing cattle.'

Which he undoubtedly was, Dane thought.

'He said that McGraw needed to be taught a lesson. He hated McGraw. I didn't like him so much myself,' Rita added. Dane had noted that everything she said blamed Frank Baker for her actions, as if she were only a puppet, or a fool in love. Dane doubted it. The woman was too cunning to be deceived by Baker's small romantic artifices.

'So you went on calmly serving poison to Calvin McGraw?' Roberta asked in disbelief. How could this little maid be such a heartless killer?

'It was only supposed to make Mr McGraw sick,' Rita lied, opening her eyes wide in a wasted plea for belief, 'while Frank showed how important he was to the ranch.'

'And later?' Dane asked.

'And later, after Mr McGraw had passed away, Frank told me that the job was half done. He was that much closer to owning the Double M.'

'With only Kent Madison and Roberta standing in his way.'

'Oh, Miss Roberta,' Rita said disparagingly. 'Frank, he said she is nothing to worry about. She knows nothing about running a ranch anyway. She will probably leave

109

after her father is gone.'

Roberta didn't even take offense, she just shook her head at the depths of Rita's perfidy. 'So you set out to poison my father as well.'

'I did not like to!' Rita said. 'Mr Madison was always good to us – me and Carlos – but now things had gone too far. Frank said that he would give me over to the law if I did not go along with him.'

Neither Dane nor Roberta believed the woman's pathetic excuses, her sad expression. She might have been encouraged by Baker, but she had been forced into nothing. Rita looked to Dane for sympathy, perhaps believing that he would be an easier target for her pitiable self.

'What can I do now, Mr Hollister?' she asked, spreading her hands. Her eyes were moist with insincere tears, In his time Dane had been influenced by a woman's tears, Not this time. He stood and told her deliberately,

'Take the bargain you have been given: leave this house within half an hour,' Dane said, trying to control the disgust in his voice.

Rita rose, straightened her dark skirt and said, 'If there is something for me in the will—'

Dane cut her off. 'Get out! Now!'

Rita's eyes went fearful, then turned challenging, but she scuttled away toward her room as Dane stood fuming. Roberta rose to cling to his arm.

'I shouldn't let her get off this lightly,' Roberta said.

'What she's done cannot be undone,' Dane said. 'Vengeance is more trouble than it's worth, Let her live out her life of despicable depravity.'

Roberta glanced up at Dane who stood unmoving, his jaw set and furious. He came out with the strangest words at the oddest of times. She remembered once hearing someone – Sparky? – call him 'Professor'. It was, she thought, as though Dane had moderated his language once he found himself among rough cowhands and men of little education, not wanting them to think that he was high-hatting them.

'If only you did not dislike Emily Dickinson,' Roberta said incongruously. Dane frowned, taken aback by Roberta's sudden shift of thoughts.

'I did not say that,' he said, turning Roberta with both of his hands on her shoulders so that she was forced to look directly up into his eyes. 'I have a volume of her poetry, do I not? I only said that I thought she must have been a very lonely woman.'

And Roberta, weary with the day and the troubles of the Double M, sagged forward a little and rested in his arms. They were barely aware of Rita Real as she ran down the stairway, a suitcase in hand and fled toward the back door of the house.

Sparky awoke stiff but feeling that he might actually survive as the new sun reddened the few glass windows of the bunkhouse. Hal Kramer and Jake Allison, having been up all night with the herd, were fast asleep on their bunks. Cooky had boiled a gallon pot of coffee and made some flapjacks before returning to his work, unloading the unused trail supplies from the chuck wagon, putting them back in the house larder with Carlos's aid.

' 'Morning,' Sparky said, spying Tango near the stove, sipping coffee. Sparky rubbed his head, his eyes, and started to rise, but his legs would not support him. Tango watched. 'It'll take me a minute to get my blood going,'

Sparky apologized.

'Want me to bring you a cup of coffee?' Tango asked.

'I can. . . . Sure, Tango. Thanks.'

'Feeling any better?'

'A lot,' Sparky said though considering the shape he had been in, that wasn't saying much. He took the white ceramic cup filled with hot strong coffee from Tango and said, 'You look as if you're ready to ride this morning.'

'I am,' Tango replied. 'I thought I'd go up to Mammoth Point and have a look-around.'

'I'll go with you,' Sparky volunteered, again trying to rise.

'I'm taking Leland,' Tango told him. 'You help out around the ranch.'

'Leland?' Sparky looked hurt. 'I'll be all right once I'm in leather, Tango.'

'Look, Sparky, I appreciate the offer, but I'd rather have Toby with me. He's fit as well as willing.'

'All right,' Sparky said sullenly, sitting on his cot again. 'Where's Dane?'

'Haven't seen him.'

'Well, if you do, ask him what he wants me to do.'

'I already know what he'd tell you,' Tango said with a smile. Both men said the word at once:

'Rest?'

It was true that Tango had not seen Dane, but when he had awakened after a night's heavy sleep he had found a note pinned to his blanket. It was from Dane Hollister. It read:

'Found Madison's will. Roberta and I are off to Dos Picos to take care of legal matters.'

When Toby Leland returned to the bunkhouse, having

112

saddled his own roan and Tango's sorrel, he glanced at Sparky moodily. It was obvious which of the young men wanted to accompany Tango to Mammoth Point, equally obvious which of them was capable of it.

Leland took a section of waxed paper from Cooky's cupboard, spread it on the table and placed half a dozen warm hot-cakes on it. He folded the package neatly as Sparky eyed him with amusement.

'Going on a picnic, Toby?'

'Might not eat for a while,' Leland answered grumpily. 'We aren't all going to be sitting around in the bunkhouse today.'

'Are you about ready?' Tango asked, picking up his Winchester from where it had rested next to his bunk.

'All ready,' Leland said dismally. Tango almost felt like telling the kid to stay behind if he wasn't up to it, but he always liked someone to cover his back in situations like this. The choice had narrowed down to Leland or no one at all. They had agreed to leave the working cowhands out of this. They were needed to watch the herd. Who knew if Baker, in a sudden fury might descend on the ranch and try to take the cattle again, perhaps with a new band of recruited toughs. Besides, Kramer and Allison had just crawled into their bunks, Gomez and Sully would have their hands full even on an uneventful day caring for the 600 steers on the range. Dane had pointed out that the Double M was still working with half a crew. The Rose Canyon gang had been of no help on day-to-day chores.

How would Dane and Roberta fare? Tango wondered, but it did nothing to alter his plan.

Tango had his own job to worry about. Make sure that the Gage & Company loggers hadn't swarmed into the timber up along the Point.

And there was Jeb Fry to consider. Tango did not think there was any way out of this that didn't include facing down the gunfighter. He knew Fry's reputation as Fry knew his. They had crossed paths once in Yuma prison, meeting without ever really speaking. The story of the nose-shooting duel was circulated far and wide, giving Fry the reputation as not only quick, but a deadly accurate marksman. Tango wasn't concerned with rumors. He supposed he really didn't need his nose anyway, and it was unlikely that if they met Jeb Fry would be aiming for such a small part of his anatomy.

Sparky sat on his bunk with his coffee mug between his hands, watching as Tango prepared to leave.

As Drew Tango placed his hat on his head and turned to go, Sparky spoke up.

'Tango?'

'What is it?' Tango asked without turning around.

'Don't cut it too fine. It won't work with Jeb Fry.'

By which he meant he knew that Tango wished never again to have to shoot to kill, but Jeb Fry was not going to wait to have an axe shot out of his hand, his knee take a bullet. Jeb Fry was quick and good. When he drew, if he drew, he was going to shoot meaning fully to kill Tango. This was no time for sideshow shooting, for showing mercy. Not if Tango was going to survive. Tango only nodded his response and strode toward the door of the bunkhouse where a nervous Toby Leland waited, mounted, holding the reins to Tango's horse.

'Ready?' Tango asked as he swung into leather. Leland nodded his answer, but he certainly didn't look eager. You couldn't blame him. A man hired on to do a cowhand's work shouldn't be expected to face guns on a daily basis. So far Leland had done as well as could be expected.

They wove their way up the chaparral-dotted south slope of Mammoth Point, following the familiar trail toward the peak, where the heads of the tall pines could be glimpsed now. They heard no sounds of axes or saws, but then they were still far away, and the loggers would probably begin their work near the Little Legend Creek. If there were any loggers there. They did not even know that for sure.

The day was warm, but not stunningly hot as they made their way along the flank of the Mammoth. Both men drank from their canteens frequently and Leland had dipped into his stack of cold hotcakes to chew on them as they rode.

'You eat twice as much as any man I know,' Tango said.

'So?' Leland said defensively.

'Nothing.' Tango shrugged. 'It's just been pointed out that you have an obsession about food. Sparky says that after licking your plate clean, you start worrying about where your next meal is coming from.'

Leland wrapped the strap of his canteen around his saddle horn without answering. They continued in silence. Then he asked:

'Do you want to know why that is, Tango?'

'Not if you don't want to tell me.'

'I don't really mind. The boys are always ragging me about taking a few extra biscuits from the table when I leave, things like that. I never felt like telling them the whole story behind that. You see, Tango, when I was growing up on the long plains my father was a scratch-dirt farmer. Maybe he wasn't very good at it, I wouldn't know.

115

But summers we would have drought, terrible dust storms and in winter the snows came heavy. We never had a thing in our pantry. We were half-hungry most of the time. One Thanksgiving my father managed to buy a chicken for us – me, my mother and three sisters. Man, we thought that was the finest thing ever!

'It went on for year after year. Mother was skin and bones when she finally passed away. My father wasn't much better off. Two of my sisters ran away to avoid starvation. The third died of it. I stuck it out, being the man of the family.

'But the land was dead and I knew it. It was always intended to be only buffalo grass and not to be tilled at all. When my father died, I stood looking at the dust shrouded land and I knew it was no use. I shook my head and started west. When I landed on the Double M, Kent Madison took me in. He even invited me to the big house for dinner. We had roast beef and sweet potatoes – I can still remember the entire menu. I thought I was in Paradise.

'Then I could go out and ride among all those sleek, fat cows and think about how many steaks on the hoof I was looking at. I knew the Double M was the place for me. I didn't care what Kent Madison was paying me, just so that I knew I would never have to go hungry again.'

'Sorry if I was prying,' Tango said.

'It's all right, Tango. It's just that I was loyal to the Double M from the first day, that's why it rattled me so much to get fired by Frank Baker. Then when I found myself out on the desert without much food, the old thoughts returned to me like daytime nightmares.'

Tango nodded. He knew all about daytime nightmares. Only his involved innocent blood. He could almost justify the killing of an innocent man by telling himself that Thatcher was a thug anyway, but it didn't work. Whatever he was, Thatcher had just been a man who had bought a ticket on a train going somewhere – maybe to commit a crime, maybe to try for a better life. And a drunken gun had shot him down. . . .

They had crested out the ridge and sat their ponies, letting them blow. Far below them the Little Legend, seeming slow, lazy and silver blue on this morning, flowed southward past the point.

Looking through the stands of bluish pine trees, Leland could see no activity.

'See anything?' he asked Tango.

'Thought I did, briefly. If they came in canoes this time, they've drawn them up into the trees. But I'm pretty sure I saw some movement.'

'They're sure not lumbering. We'd see a lot of activity, or hear the axes by now.'

'Maybe they're holding off until Gage gives them the go-ahead. He must be questioning the validity of the deal he made with Baker by now.'

'You think so?' Leland looked hopeful.

'I don't know. Unless Gage wanted to ride overland, and I don't take him for that kind of man, the only way to reach the Mammoth is via Dos Picos. Dane might have caught up with him already.' On the way up the mountain he had already told Leland about Dane's having somehow found Kent Madison's will.

'I hope that does the trick,' Leland said. 'At least that doesn't seem to be a full-blown timber camp down there.'

'No. But there still might be a few point men, like that one-eyed rascal. More to the point, Frank Baker might be

117

down there himself, checking things out.'

And where he went the gunman, Jeb Fry, was sure to be found.

'Let's get a little closer, Leland. Keep your eyes wide open and keep that Winchester of yours handy.'

TEN

Dane Hollister had never seen an enraged walrus. In fact he had never seen a walrus at all. But just now Wesley Gage, owner of Gage and Company, was giving Dane a fair idea of what one might look like. A big man – robust he liked to call himself – Gage had a thick, flowing mustache and sagging jowls.

They were in the chambers of Judge Thomas, who seemed only a little more impressive in his robe than he did otherwise. His pink cheeks were slick with a new shave and he gave the impression of being a grown-up, well-fed baby. Nevertheless the man was the arbiter of the law in Dos Picos and for 500 miles around.

Roberta sat beside Dane in a wooden chair. They watched as Gage performed a few antics, slapping his arms, spinning on his toes as he shouted at the judge, restrained himself as Thomas frowned, and tried beseeching the court.

Through a high window morning sun slanted into the room, trailing a comet's tail of dust motes. Judge Thomas waited until Gage was finished with his performance, then said quietly, but sternly:

'You should have been more cautious, Mr Gage. I would think that a man with your business experience—'

'Mr Baker represented himself as the business manager of Double M Ranch,' Gage, now perspiring, almost shouted. Thomas frowned. He had had enough of Gage's blustering and flapping about.

'Did you ask to see his authorization?'

Gage shrugged the question off as of no importance. 'Your Honor, I have hired thirty loggers and support staff, have contracted with a rafter to transport the cut timber.' He held up chubby fingers to count on. 'I have myself taken a loan to complete this project. I have had to pay for horses, food, tents and equipment, all of which are to be transported to the site on Mammoth Point at considerable expense.'

'All the more reason you should have assured yourself of Frank Baker's authority,' Judge Thomas said. 'Did you ever personally speak to Kent Madison, owner of the Double M?'

'I was told that he was very ill, that he was allowed no visitors. That was why Baker was conducting his affairs.'

'And the person who told you that was?'

'Frank Baker!' Gage said, lifting his voice to a shout again. In a way, Dane couldn't blame the man for being furious. He was about to take a financial bath.

Dane had to restrain Roberta with his eyes and occasional pressure on her hand, She was nearly as excited and angry as Wesley Gage. The judge lowered his eyes, pushed his spectacles up on his nose, shook his head and looked again at Gage.

'I have had time to examine Kent Madison's will. There is absolutely no contingency which would allow Frank

Baker to act as his agent.'

'Maybe the will is a forgery!' Gage tried.

'This document was witnessed by three prominent citizens of the valley, Mr Gage. I'm sorry, I'm afraid I have to conclude that you have simply been swindled. I realize that this is going to cost you heavily, but I can do nothing.'

'But there is no justice in it!'

'Maybe not, but that is the law,' Thomas said, placing the will aside. 'People out here on the fringes of civilization have often complained that it is time to put an end to frontier justice. They insist that they want the law out here, real law. When they get it, however, they are affronted if it does not agree with their own opinions.' Thomas sighed heavily and lightly tapped his gavel.

'I hereby order Gage and Company immediately to desist and refrain from taking timber from the area known as Mammoth Point, as said property is the freehold of the Double M Ranch and no such rights to the timber have been granted.'

Gage went red in the face and was momentarily rigid. Then he paled, his eyes seemed to brighten. He turned to Roberta, wearing as polite a face as a walrus can put on.

'Perhaps, Miss Madison, something can be worked out between the two of us? I have much invested in that timber.'

'Perhaps,' Roberta said, rising. 'But not now. Certainly not before the will is probated, and I doubt that I will ever give my authorization to clear-cut that timber. Or to have you be a party to it,' she added, freezing Gage's insincere smile. 'I just don't need the money that bad.'

Gage made a few rumbling sounds, then, with fresh hope, turned toward the judge. 'Your honor, I must insist that Frank Baker's bank account be frozen.'

Thomas hesitated, pursed his lips, then nodded. 'If the contents of that account are shown to be ill-gotten gains, then your request is justified. You are ordered to return with any and all records – your own or the bank's – to prove just how much money was given to Frank Baker for attempting an illegal transaction of Double M property. I will make a final decision on the ownership of the monies then. For now, the account is not available to Mr Baker. The bank shall be so informed and so ordered.'

Thomas ended the proceedings with another polite little tap of his gavel. Gage didn't look pleased, really, but he had ended the hearing on a high note of sorts. He had at least gotten his revenge on Frank Baker. The man would not profit from the swindle.

Three hours later a disappointed and angry Wesley Gage had made his way to the base of Mammoth Pont via the northern trail, His one-eyed gang boss, Pepper was there to take the reins of the buggy horse and help his over-weight employer down. Pepper didn't have to ask how things were going; the expression on the timber man's broad face told all. Gage mopped his perspiration-streaked face with a foppish little kerchief and told Pepper:

'It's all off.'

Pepper, who had already figured as much, simply nodded. 'Good thing I didn't have the second crew transported upriver.'

'Yes, it's a good thing,' Gage said sharply, as if all of it were Pepper's fault. What was he going to do about the rafting contract? About the mule teams? About his suppliers who had already extended him credit to purchase supplies: food, tents, tools? What was he supposed to do about the extra men he already had on his payroll? What was he to do about . . . Frank Baker!

Frank Baker swaggered toward Gage from the depths of the pine forest. Beside and behind him was the bearded man Gage had started to think of as Baker's shadow, Jeb Fry.

'What are you doing here!' Gage demanded.

Frank Baker smiled enough to elevate his thin dark mustache. 'Why shouldn't I be here, Gage? This is Double M land.'

'Yes, I know that,' Gage said, sputtering. 'I would think that it's the last place you would want to be found. If Double M hands don't lynch you, you'll be thrown into the jail in Dos Picos.'

'What are you talking about? I only came here to accept the second payment. You told me that after you had a crew actually on the land—'

'Are you insane!' Gage said. 'Second payment? You'll never even be allowed to retain the first.'

'What do you mean?' Frank Baker asked, stepping nearer. Behind him his gunslick watched, hand resting on his revolver. Pepper also watched, uncertainly. He felt a loyalty toward his boss, but he did not like the way things were shaping up. 'If you think you can pull a fast one on me—'

'Me!' Gage exploded. 'You're the one who was trying a swindle. They found Kent Madison's will, Baker. It said nothing about you being authorized to manage the Double M.'

'That's a lie!'

123

'I saw it. The judge reviewed it. You're nothing but a cheat and a liar, Baker.'

Baker tensed. Pepper tried to move farther aside. He knew that his boss had gone too far.

Baker asked, 'Who says they found the will?'

'His daughter showed up in the judge's chambers with it this morning.'

'It can't be,' Baker said, shaking his head. He and Rita had practically torn the big house apart, searching for it. Baker had been convinced that there was no such document to be found, Unless Rita. . . ? Did the girl have the nerve to cross him? Perhaps making a deal with Roberta Madison for a part of Kent Madison's fortune? It seemed unlikely – not that silly, trusting wench.

'It's so,' Gage answered. 'If you've any sense you'll ride out of this territory now.'

'I came for payment; I'll have it.'

'I haven't got any money to offer, and if I had you would have to pry it from my dead hand!' Gage exclaimed. Then he did the last thing anyone would have expected from the fat lumber company man; he reached into his vest pocket and came up with a twin-barrelled .40 caliber derringer.

It was a desperate move for a man unused to guns and gunplay. Sunlight struck the small pistol, revealing it for what it was, and Frank Baker thrust himself to one side and drew his Colt. Two shots roared out – both of them from Frank Baker's revolver. Gage was driven back against the horse drawing his buggy and he slid to the earth as the panicked animal danced away. Pepper stood with his hands half-raised, watching the life seep out of Gage.

'How will you have it?' Frank Baker demanded of Pepper.

124

'Can I get my canoe?'

'Get it and take the corpse with you,' Baker said gruffly. He still had not holstered his weapon.

'What are we going to do now?' Jeb Fry asked as he stepped up beside Baker, It was not an anxious question; there was little that could rattle Fry. He had watched the episode almost with boredom, certainly with detachment, paying attention only to Baker's technique in drawing and firing. You never knew when a friend might become an enemy. Baker, he decided, was competent. A little slow, but then maybe that was because of his adversary's obvious lack of skill.

'Dos Picos,' Baker said. 'I've got money in the bank there. Or should I say *we* have money there,' he added, trying to cement Jeb Fry's loyalty.

Jeb Fry had loyalty to the cause, of course. That is, to the money. That was his motivation for working with Baker from the first. If there was to be no more of it, then he would ride with Frank Baker while he recovered his money. After that, he thought shrugging mentally, a lot of things could happen to Frank Baker on the trail. Jeb Fry felt that he had already been cheated through Frank Baker's incompetence. But double his cut would almost be enough to satisfy his outrage.

'You heard that?' Toby Leland asked unnecessarily as he and Tango wove their way along the northern flank of Mammoth Point, surrounded by virgin pines. Tango nodded. It was hard to mistake the sharp bark of a .44. 'What do you think?'

'I think we have to have a look,' Tango replied. 'But I think we ought to approach cautiously.'

One gun, fired twice. It sounded a lot like murder. Whose, and why it might have been done, he could not guess. His first thought, of course, was Jeb Fry; Tango was still convinced that there was no way out of this that did not involve a face-down with the bearded gunman.

They emerged from the thick pine forest into the timber camp to find no one around. No one, that is, except for Wesley Gage, who lay crumpled in the sandy soil along the Little Legend, a derringer not far from his inert fingers, two bullet holes neatly spaced on his vest.

'Who do you think did it?' Leland asked as they crouched over the body.

'It had to be Baker or Jeb Fry, don't you think?' Tango answered, rising to dust his hands together. 'It certainly wasn't one of Gage's own men. Why kill your source of income?'

'Same thing goes with Frank Baker, doesn't it?' Leland asked.

'Unless Gage wasn't going to pay him any more. We don't know what happened in Dos Picos, but it could be that Dane and Roberta set Gage wise – and unwittingly signed his death warrant. See if you can find the tracks of the killers, Leland. I'll put Gage in the back of his buggy. Or, wait – he's a big man, you'd better help me first.'

With Leland driving the buggy, his own pony tied on behind, they started along the north road toward Dos Picos. It was a seldom traveled route, leading nowhere, and so it was easy enough to pick up the fresh tracks in the clay soil. The wheels of Gage's hired buggy showed clearly from his morning ride to meet his own destiny. And the tracks of the riders departing the logging camp were plain. Horses not moving fast, but steadily back toward

Dos Picas.

Tango was frowning. Briefly he had drawn his sorrel up beside the road. Leland held up the buggy and asked Tango:

'What's the matter, Drew?'

'There's a third horseman,' Tango said. They had known, or at least strongly suspected, that Baker and Jeb Fry were at the logging camp and responsible for the killing of Gage, but the third rider was a mystery.

'You and Dane Hollister both said that there was one gunman missing after we ran off Hummel and Sturgis.'

'Yes, there was a man unaccounted for,' Tango answered thoughtfully. 'There were four hired men, we know that. Who is this one, and what is he doing?'

'Maybe he's what you would call an ace in the hole,' Leland suggested. 'Someone to watch Baker's back in case Jeb Fry tries to turn on him.'

'Or Jeb Fry's ace,' Tango said. 'In case Baker tries to cheat Fry out of his cut. That seems more likely. This man, whoever hc is, he rode in with Fry.'

Either way, they would do well to keep a sharp eye out for the unknown man. For now, they had to reach Dos Picos speedily. Dane and Roberta were still there, presumably, and Frank Baker might be on the verge of losing control. His plans were unraveling rapidly, and he had always been a violent and unpredictable man.

At that moment, unaware of the trouble up along the Little Legend, Roberta and Dane were feeling quite proud of themselves. They had recovered Kent Madison's will, chased off the cattle thieves, shot down the timber company belonging to Wesley Gage and now were in the process of driving the final nail into Frank Baker's coffin.

Amos Blount lifted his sad watery eyes to them, placed the court order aside and nodded. 'Judge Thomas has ordered that the assets of Frank Baker be frozen, Personally I think it is the proper decision, under the circumstances. I suppose that money now reverts to Gage and Company. Judge Thomas has subpoenaed all of our records having to do with Mr Baker's account.' He shrugged. 'You already know all of that; what else can I do for you?'

'We were wondering,' Dane said, 'about any large deposits going back further – years perhaps. It's all well and good that Gage gets his money back, but we also suspect that Frank Baker has been stealing Double M cattle and selling them over a long period of time. Calvin McGraw once accused Baker of doing just that, and we believe that this is what led to his murder.'

'McGraw was murdered as well?' Blount said incredulously.

'Poisoned.'

Blount took a moment to compose himself. He wedged the thick fingers of his hands together and leaned back. Thoughtfully he said, 'It did seem to me that the Double M was not as prosperous as it once had been, judging from Kent Madison's deposits. But that could have been blamed on any of the vagaries of ranching – drought, freeze, overgrazing. But if I considered it in the light of what we now know about Frank Baker, his personal account did seem to be growing well. I didn't think much of it at the time. I considered that perhaps he had been earning periodic raises or bonuses as ranch foreman, or that he simply had become more frugal. People do change their savings

128

patterns, you know. What would you like me to do?'

'We know that only Judge Thomas can order you to freeze those funds, and we have no proof that some of it was earned by rustling cattle, much as we suspect it. But we ask,' Dane said leaning forward, 'that you examine those deposits, the amounts and timing of them; for example, if they were made at or near round-up time, it would show a pattern of profits that we might be able to petition the court to have returned to the Double M.'

'Do you have any idea how much work is involved in this?' Blount asked.

'I think so,' Dane said rising and offering his arm to Roberta. 'But we would be extremely grateful.'

'And you would have a loyal depositor for as long as Double M exists,' Roberta said, smiling sweetly.

Dane didn't know if it was the promise of Double M's loyalty to the bank – the ranch was one of the largest accounts Amos Blount had – or Roberta's suddenly girlish charm that did the trick, but Blount, without standing, waved his hands and asked them to leave his office, saying:

'I have a lot of paperwork to do.'

Halfway to the front door with the nervous Mr Preston watching from behind the grille of his teller's station, Dane halted Roberta and turned her to face him.

'Do you want to get married today? he asked.

'Do I . . . what? Are you joking, Dane!'

'No,' he replied. 'I'm quite serious.'

'But you can't be. . . .' Their eyes met and stayed locked for a long half-minute before Roberta let her gaze fade and she shook her head.

'No. No, Dane, I don't want to marry you . . . today.'

Which left him with a faint hope, but little encouragement. Feeling rebuffed, slightly embarrassed, he tried to lighten the mood.

'Has this anything to do with Emily Dickinson?'

He was grinning as he said that, but Roberta answered with a straight face and a small shake of her head.

'No. No, Dane, it doesn't.'

He wondered then, as a man refused does, what it could be. Was she just not ready? There was no one else in her life that he knew of. Was it just that he wasn't much to look at, nothing but a typical cowboy, only another pony ornament in scuffed boots and faded jeans?

Or was she still thinking of the story of his being a murderer? Perhaps she had not believed or understood his explanation of how the young man in Austin had died under his knife.

Of course it could have been much simpler: she just didn't care for him in that way. That would be the hardest explanation to swallow.

Mr Preston, from his teller's station, asked:

'Is there something more we can do for you two?'

'No,' Dane said, letting his hands slide from Roberta's shoulder. 'I don't think there's anything anyone can do.'

Dane opened the front door to the bank, squinting as his eyes met the blue-white glare of the desert sun. The bulky figure of a man appeared in the doorway, casting a shadow over them. Dane started to apologize and step back.

Then he recognized Frank Baker.

ELEVEN

Dane Hollister staggered back as Frank Baker shouldered him roughly into the bank and spun Roberta aside with one hand. Dane reached down, but it was too late, Baker had slicked his Colt away before Dane knew what was happening.

'Just back up,' Baker ordered. Behind him Dane could make out Jeb Fry standing at the hitchrail, holding the leads to two horses. The dry wind whispered past, drifting light sand up the main street. Opposite, at a diagonal, was Marshal Morgan Teal's office, but the door stood closed, and no one seemed to be there.

'What is it?' Roberta asked with fire. 'What do you want, you murderer!'

Baker didn't answer. There was the salt and pepper of beard on his face now, causing his pencil-thin mustache to appear slightly ridiculous. Normally well-groomed, Frank had spent much time away from the comforts of home lately.

'What's all this!' Amos Blount demanded, appearing from his back office with a sheaf of papers in his hand, his vest unbuttoned. 'Oh, it's you, Baker.'

'It's me. I just need to make a withdrawal,' Baker said. He still held Dane Hollister's pistol loosely in his hand. The sight wasn't lost on Blount who frowned and answered:

'I'm sorry, Mr Baker. You see, Judge Thomas has frozen your account until certain irregularities can be examined.'

'Oh, that's all right,' Frank Baker said equably. Blount seemed to relax a little before Baker added, 'I'll just take it all, then.'

'All. . . ?' Blount said.

'Start filling up sacks,' Baker said, now holding the pistol level, aiming it directly at Blount. 'Do it! And if your teller there has a gun, tell him not to make a mistake and go for it, or I'll kill you.'

'You're making a huge blunder, Baker,' Blount said, although with a hand gesture he had ordered Preston to start filling money sacks with the cash from his till. 'If you'll just be patient . . . the court hasn't yet decided that the money is not rightfully yours.'

'Now I don't have to wait for the judge to decide.'

'You're piling one crime on top of the other, Baker – and bank robbery!' Blount tried. 'They'll track you down and hang you.'

'What would they do anyway?' Baker almost laughed. 'They're going to try to hang me for the murder of Kent Madison, isn't that right, Roberta? Dane?'

'They'd have a tough time proving it,' Dane said, trying to calm Baker, for now he saw that the man was desperately dangerous. Baker seemed to feel that he had nothing else to lose – what would his next step be?

'Would they?' Baker sneered. 'What about little Rita? I'll bet she's already cracked, confessed, hasn't she?'

No one answered, giving Baker all the confirmation that he needed.

'She's gone,' Roberta tried.

'And she can be found and brought back,' Baker said. 'I'm not taking the chance of hanging! And they'll stumble across Gage, too,' he blurted out.

'Gage?' Blount asked, stunned.

'It doesn't matter now. Yes – hurry up with those money sacks, Preston – Gage is dead.'

Dane thought quickly. Tango had been headed to the timberland, but Baker hadn't mentioned him. So, Dane thought, Tango was still alive and probably on Baker's trail. Unless he had somehow failed to receive Dane's note.

'It's all your fault, Dane,' Baker said as be scooped up the first of three moneybags from a petrified, white-faced Preston. 'All of it! You came out here and tried to take over everything. I watched you polishing up Kent Madison—'

'I sincerely liked Kent,' Dane interrupted, but Baker seemed not even to hear him.

'You wanted the Double M for yourself – and all of its possessions. Including Roberta! I saw that from the first, too. When I told Kent that you were stalking his daughter, he brushed the thought aside. But I didn't! Why do you think I fired you? I knew you were getting ready to make your move to claim the Double M one way or the other – even if it took courting Miss Roberta here.'

'That's not true, Baker,' Dane said. Again his words went unheard by the out of control Frank Baker. Roberta had Dane's hand now, and she squeezed it in terror as the light in Baker's eyes grew wilder and somehow darker.

133

Jeb Fry had entered the bank for the first time. Now he made 'hurry-up' gestures to Frank who tossed the bearded badman the bags of money.

'Let's go, Frank! I thought I saw someone stirring in the marshal's office,' Fry told him.

'All right,' Frank Baker said, his chest heaving with what he considered righteous indignation. 'You,' he said, motioning toward Preston with his pistol. 'Come out of there. Hollister, Blount, and you, teller, all of you on your faces on the floor. Now!'

Roberta started to join the men as they lay on the floor, but Frank Baker stopped her, 'Not you, Miss Madison – you're going to take a little ride with us.'

'Bad idea, Frank,' Jeb Fry said.

'No, it's not. If they send anyone after us, they won't want to start shooting around the woman.'

Fry nodded, although neither he nor anyone else believed that this was the sole reason Frank Baker was taking Roberta with him. He had wanted Double M, and all of its 'possessions', and that included Roberta Madison. What he had not succeeded in getting through subterfuge, he was determined to take by force of arms.

'Frank,' Jeb Fry prodded.

'All right – let's go, Roberta. Hollister, the only reason I'm not going to shoot you dead is that I don't care to bring the marshal running. If you dare to come after me, it will be the end of you – and possibly of the little woman here. I'd advise you to consider that deeply before you do anything foolish.'

'Frank!' Jeb Fry implored from his saddle and Baker started that way, towing Roberta after him. Her eyes met Dane's briefly and seemed to beg of him, *Don't try coming after us, Dane!*

There was no chance of that happening.

After a minute they heard the sound of horses racing away up the street.

'Get the marshal!' Blount yelled, rising from the floor, and Preston lit out, moving faster than Dane would have suspected the bank teller was capable of. He sprinted across the street, coat tails flying. Dane went out into the hot sunshine, glanced around and muttered a small curse. The robbers had taken his buckskin horse along with them, no doubt to delay pursuit.

'Aren't you going to wait for the marshal!' Blount asked as Dane started off determinedly toward Tonio's stable.

'He can talk to me later,' Dane said. He needed a horse, and needed it now. He walked the two blocks to Tonio's to find a cluster of men standing around a buggy. Marshal Morgan Teal was among them, as was Toby Leland and Tango. Now what!

Nearing the buggy he could see the dead man it held, and recognized him by his walrus mustache. Taking the heavy Tonio by the arm Dane turned him away and said, 'I need a horse Tonio, and now – a fast one.'

'What is it, Dane?' he heard Tango ask.

'Baker's got Roberta,' Dane said.

'What? How. . . ?'

The marshal had heard that and he started that way. 'Frank Baker?' he asked. Teal had a murdered man and a kidnapping on the same day. It was no way to start a hot Tuesday morning. Dane answered the marshal.

'Baker took her. He just robbed the bank.'

Teal's face grew longer. Three major crimes to handle at once. Teal wasn't equipped to handle trouble in bunches. He was a town marshal and was used to breaking up fights and throwing drunken troublemakers in jail; that was about it.

Tonio had emerged with a tall paint pony for Dane. Dane took the reins and said to the marshal: 'Baker killed Wesley Gage. He confessed to it in front of me, Blount and Preston.'

'Did he?' What was Baker: a one-man crime spree? Teal said shakily, 'I'll talk to Amos Blount and try raising a posse. The three of you stick around – I want to talk to you some more.'

'Later,' Dane said, swinging aboard the paint pony. 'Want to go, Tango? They've got Jeb Fry with them.'

'Try to stop me,' Tango said. 'Leland, you can stay and—'

'No,' Toby Leland said stubbornly, and he mounted his roan horse. 'I'll not be left out. Miss Roberta would expect the Rose Canyon gang to come after her.'

No one argued; there wasn't the time for it anyway. Frank Baker had a pretty good lead on them by now, He would find out soon enough that he had made a mistake in taking Dane's slow-moving buckskin with him, but they could simply cut the horse loose and continue if it slowed them. They needed it for nothing; it had only been taken to try to keep Dane off their back trail.

The three heeled their ponies toward the head of town, leaving a trail of white sifting dust. Dane caught a glimpse of Marshal Teal, still looking overwhelmed by the morning's events, scratching his head in confusion as he watched them ride.

'Which way do you think they'll go?' Tango shouted as the horses pounded on.

136

'I don't know. You'd think straight toward Tucson, but Frank Baker knows this country better than any of us. He might decide to try to lose his trail in rough country.'

There would be a posse, of course. The townsmen would be howling mad that the bank had been robbed, but by the time Teal had gathered his posse and started on his way Baker would be hours ahead of them. If Tucson was his destination, he could even have the time to take a railroad train out of the territory.

All of that was unimportant to Dane. He had to track Baker down before he could get that far. He didn't even care just then if Frank Baker got away with the money. He had to make sure that Roberta was safe.

For mile after mile the three pursuers did not speak. With the jolting horses beneath them, speech was nearly impossible anyway at full speed. They did, however, eventually have to slow the horses. The sand was growing deeper; the sun rose higher and the desert heat assailed them. Tonio was a good man, but he hadn't thought to put a canteen on Dane's rig.

'How about a little water, Tango?' he asked as they slowed their horses to a walk. Tango handed over his canteen.

'I was hoping to catch them quick,' Tango said, cuffing at his brow. 'Looks like we've got a long hot trail ahead of us.'

'So it seems,' Dane said despondently.

'Did Baker really confess to killing Gage?'

'He did. Bragged about it, more or less. I suppose Gage told him that he knew Baker's claim of representing the Double M was a lie. Gage was no diplomat; he probably told Baker the wrong way and Frank lashed out. Frank knew that he had lost the cattle sale, now he had lost the timber deal as well. He couldn't go back to the ranch. Rita Real had already implicated him in the murders of both Calvin McGraw and Kent Madison. He had to make his run, and he didn't mean to go empty-handed.'

'The man's a vulture,' Toby Leland said savagely. He took a sip of water from his own canteen. 'Look how many people he's harmed.'

'And he'll keep on living like that,' Tango believed.

'No he won't,' Dane Hollister promised. 'I won't let him.'

Toby rose slightly in his stirrups, then stood up in them. He was pointing southward across the long white-sand desert.

'What is it, Toby?'

'There's a horse up there. Just standing with its head down.'

Peering that way against the white sun and the heat veils, the others now saw what Toby had seen. Dane's heart sank. What if Frank had simply decided that taking Roberta along was too difficult and . . . left her behind. Without a word passing between them, the three men heeled their horse into rapid motion, Tango now holding his Winchester in his hand.

What they found at the end of the hard ride was not what they had expected or feared. Dane Hollister's buckskin horse looked up at them curiously and then began munching on some scattered mesquite beans it had found beneath an isolated thorn tree. Dane cursed.

'I should have known. The old rascal is slow-witted and slow-footed. Must have given them too much trouble.' Even as he was talking, Dane was swinging down from the saddle, working at the cinches.

'What are you doing? We're wasting time,' Toby Leland complained.

'I'm getting a fresh horse under me,' Dane replied. 'I might need one, and I guarantee you I know how to make the old sluggard run.'

The paint pony was turned loose to either follow after them or return to Dos Picos. It seemed it had had enough of desert running, for they saw it trotting away toward Tonio's distant, familiar stable.

The buckskin rolled its eyes, and if a horse could moan, it nearly moaned at the thought of having its harsh taskmaster back. Dane touched spurs to the reluctant horse, and the buckskin knew Dane meant business; and this was no time for playing one of his games.

To the west now a low, broken line of dark hills appeared. A place of tangled canyons and broken land-forms, it was known locally as the Pima range. Tango watched the hills rise and fall, fold and break off upon each other.

'Do you think Baker went up into the Pima badlands?' he asked.

'I don't know,' Dane said irritably.

'It would take an army to find him and get him out of there.'

Leland commented, 'If I was him, I'd be heading for Tucson. Getting out of the country as soon as possible.'

'Frank Baker's proved himself to be a patient man,' Dane answered. 'Look how long he worked his plan to take over the Double M.'

'Jeb Fry might not be,' Tango said. 'He's sort of a sudden man. He'll want his cut of the bank money, then he'll blow out of the territory before a posse can be mounted to track them down.'

'You seem to know a lot about Jeb Fry?' Dane said, a question in his eyes. Tango only nodded and said:

'I could be wrong, but Fry lives by his wits. A quick payday and then vanish again. He's not like Frank Baker, taking years to poison McGraw and Madison, stealing their cattle, setting up the timber deal with Gage. No, Baker meant to take over the Double M and settle there. Jeb Fry is a hired gun, plain and simple. It's all he's ever been, all he ever will be. A man of little patience.'

They discussed it no further. What they needed, now that the sun was beginning to wheel over toward the western hills where shadows were lengthening at the base of the Pimas, was to find the tracks of the bandits. They couldn't afford to make the mistake of assuming that Baker and Fry had ridden toward Tucson and so pass them by as they concealed themselves in some hidden canyon in the Pimas. Nor could they ride into the Pimas and waste their time searching the vast wasteland as Baker, his pockets filled with gold, escaped on a fast train from Tucson.

They spread out looking for tracks. The sun was still shining in the western skies, but its glow was blocked by the Pimas where deep purple shadows were gathering in the canyons and clefts. If they didn't find some sign of Baker and his party soon, it would be too late for tracking.

Perhaps too late for Roberta.

'I think I've got 'em!' Leland shouted out. He whistled sharply and waved an arm, bringing Dane and Tango on the run. 'Right there,' Leland said. He had swung down from his saddle to indicate the tracks of three horses

140

which had briefly passed over hard pan before entering the sands again.

'That's the built-up right rear shoe of Roberta's gray,' Leland agreed.

'And the chipped shot is Frank Baker's. I've seen it on the home range for months,' Tango said. 'He was always going to have it replaced. Never did.'

Dane rose, hands on hips and looked toward the Pimas, his mouth tightening. The squat, dark jumble of tangled hills seemed impenetrable. There were a hundred feeder canyons twisting down the flanks of the black hills, a thousand roads in and perhaps none out. It would be, Dane thought, the perfect place to lay a trap. And it would be a bad place to die.

They had no choice.

'Let's ride nearer,' Tango said. 'Maybe we can pick up their tracks again once we're out of the blow sand.'

And maybe not, Dane thought grimly. There was a fury building in him that he had to work to suppress. Anger would do Roberta no good. They did not speak of it, but he knew they rode with a single purpose. Getting Roberta to safety. To hell with the bank's stolen money. Eventually there would be a posse on Frank Baker's trail. Although they likely would be too late to do much good. Let Baker keep the money; he had to give Roberta back.

The walls of the canyon they first approached loomed dark and craggy. The shadows had reclaimed the desert sky, though there was still a purple glow above the broken ridges. A coyote, surprised as it emerged from its den on a sundown hunting expedition, looked up at them, startled by their passing, and fled into the underbrush.

They halted their horses at the mouth of the narrow

canyon, searching for sign.

'I think this is the way,' Tango said, wiping at his forehead with his white scarf. It was still hot, the air unmoving around them.

'If we're wrong we could ride up in that tangle and waste hours,' Dane answered. 'We don't have much daylight left.'

'If we don't try it, we've wasted time as well,' Tango replied, his surface coolness covering his own anxiety.

'I think Tango's right,' Leland said. 'Look, here's another hoof print. I can't tell if it matches those from any of the horses we found back there or not, but it's fresh, and it's leading into the canyon.'

Dane rode to where Leland pointed at the scarred stone a horse had turned. Leland was becoming quite a tracker. Neither of the distinctive marks they had found earlier matched this one, but it seemed unlikely that anyone else had recently passed this way. There was nowhere to go in the Pimas, nothing there but dead land and dry washes, a confusion of dead-end trails. Perhaps the Indians had once lived there, but Dane did not think so. He knew of no water source to support human life across all of the badlands.

It was certain that no unshod Indian pony had made the track Leland had found. Night was settling; the cool shadows lengthened still more. In an hour it would be impossible to find any tracks, impossible to find Roberta before the cold desert night settled across the land.

'Let's give it a try, men,' Dane said and they started forward into the crazed, confusing tangle of hills with no way of knowing who or what they might find there.

142

TWELVE

'How many riders are we following?' Toby Leland asked Tango as they trailed a sullen Dane Hollister into the shadowed depths of the canyon.

'How many?'

'Yeah. We know that Jeb Fry was with Baker, but we've only found the sign of two horses,' Toby Leland said.

'Three, then,' Tango replied.

'Or four?'

'Four?' Tango said with surprise, shifting in his saddle to look at Leland.

'Remember, Tango, you told me that there was another man riding with either Baker or with Jeb Fry.'

'He wasn't at the bank. Maybe they just left him out there on his own?'

'Maybe,' Leland said doubtfully. 'I was just thinking about what you called an ace in the hole.'

'Toby,' Tango answered, 'you're a lot smarter than people give you credit for. I'd forgotten about that man, to tell you the truth.'

Leland basked in the glow of that faint praise from a man he admired. He was still a greenhorn, Leland had to admit, but he had proved that he could read sign – a little at least, and he had not forgotten the fourth man. Forgetting about him could mean death. Leland thought proudly that he had done better than Sparky could have done. His only concern about himself was the shooting . . . if it came to that, how would he handle himself?

Dane led the way along an upwardly winding trail into the darkening canyon. His buckskin horse faltered and slid backward a few feet on the slate underfooting. The animal gave its owner a reproving glance. The land to the left began to fall away steeply toward a black abyss. They had no choice but to continue, keeping close to the inner wall of the trail where stone cliffs thrust skyward.

They guided their horses along for another hundred yards or so and then found themselves on a wide bench. Here some chaparral growth prospered – manzanita, purple sage, sumac and chia. The horses stood shuddering; the heat which had been so oppressive during the first half of the ride was now being swept away by a breeze which brought a touch of chill with it. They looked down across a wild jumble of land, trackless, convoluted and dark.

'Why would Baker come up here?' Dane asked, believing now that they had been mistaken in following the canyon trail.

'Because no one but us would be crazy enough to follow him here,' Tango said, 'You know Frank Baker has been riding this country for years. What looks like an enormous puzzle to us might be familiar ground to him. I think he's decided to lie low until the searchers just give up in frustration.'

Dane was already prepared to do just that. Face it: they

144

had made a mistake. Baker and Jeb Fry were probably dining in some Tucson restaurant at this moment, laughing at the Rose Canyon gang.

'I smell smoke,' Leland said softly.

Dane's head came round in concern. If they were caught up here in the dark and a brush fire was building, they would have no chance at all. But it wasn't that. Leland was pointing toward a small valley, a pit in the darkness, it seemed, and indicating a small plume of rising smoke. A campfire. They could not see its glow, but it seemed that someone had made camp there.

'I don't see any way down there,' Tango said.

'There must be!' Dane said impatiently. 'Let's find it. I won't let Roberta spend the night with that animal.'

'Hold on,' Tango said, taking hold of the buckskin horse's bridle with one hand. 'Look, Dane, we can't even be sure that it is Baker down there. If it is, we can't go off bumbling and stumbling around in the dark. Wait a while. We've an early-rising moon these nights. Wait an hour or so and we'll be able to see something of where we are going at least.'

'All right,' Dane answered with a resigned shake of his head. 'You're right, Tango.' Dane knew that Tango was correct; however with each hour that passed without knowing that Roberta was safe, Dane was growing more anxious, more reckless, It was not the way to approach the task at hand, but he could not help feeling as he did.

'Let's let the ponies rest,' Tango told them and they swung down to sit with their backs leaning against a rock face among the brush.

The moon, when it did rise, hours later, spread a glossy sheen across the desert and invested the tangled canyon

145

with a still more puzzling aspect. Shadows merged, flowed together and screened small ravines. Dane Hollister stood, hands on hips, staring down on the landscape. The fire below them had gone out, although they could smell smoke lingering in the air.

'You know,' Tango was saying beside him, 'we don't even know if Frank Baker came up this trail, but if he did, I think I can see a way he might have gotten down there.' Tango pointed out a narrow switchback track angling down the hillside. It was lost in shadow and then would emerge into moon-bright illumination. If Tango was right, they would have to take their horses nearly fifteen feet straight down to catch the head of the trail below them.

If Tango was wrong, then the trail was just another path to nowhere among the dark, tangled hills. 'I'll tell you what,' Tango said, 'let me try to get down there with the sorrel, he's pretty sure-footed. If I make it, well, you can follow after. If you see me tumbling away. . . .' he smiled, 'then I wouldn't attempt it.'

Tango was a man with some nerve, Dane had to admit as he watched him lead his horse to the brink of the shelf, swing aboard and start the pony forward. The sorrel momentarily rolled its eyes as if his master had lost his mind, but obediently went over, slipping and sliding down the rocky face of the cliff, going nearly to its haunches as pebbles and sand fell away into the depths of the canyon.

Tango hit the narrow trail with a jolt, reined his sorrel up sharply and drew a deep breath. The drop-off below him was another 200 feet at least. Yet he waved cheerily and urged the others to follow him.

'Oh, what the heck,' Leland muttered, and with his grim face on, he followed Tango on his big roan horse, sliding down the slope to join Tango on the trail below. The buckskin, having watched the other two horses go over the cliff, not knowing their fate, gave Dane Hollister the evil eye as he walked to it and swung aboard.

'There's no choice, you stubborn oaf. We're going over,' Dane said and he touched spurs to the buckskin's flanks. After a moment's panic by both horse and rider, they slid to a halt on the end of the trail. The buckskin stood shuddering for a moment.

Tango had already gone a little way ahead, looking for a way down. Leland thought: *He'd better find one*, because there was certainly no way back up.

By the time Dane caught up with Leland Tango was already out of sight round an outside curve in the trail. The road was wide enough for the two to ride comfortably side by side, and they did, but they didn't speak to each other. They only hoped.

Rounding the bend they found Tango sitting his saddle, patting his sorrel's neck, grinning. The trail had widened to form a copse where three or four scraggly live oak trees grew.

'Men,' Tango said in a low voice as the moon through the oak trees' branches illuminated his face. 'Congratulate yourselves. If you'll look down you'll see sets of horse tracks which are familiar to you.'

'He brought Roberta that way!' Dane said angrily. 'He might have killed her.'

'The man knows these hills. He probably knows a simpler way to get down which we might have seen in full daylight. No matter,' Tango said, leaning forward, his hands crossed on the pommel of his saddle. 'He can't possibly believe that anyone could have followed him this far.

147

He won't be as wary as he would be in open country.'

'How far is their camp?' Dane wondered.

'I don't know exactly, I'd guess half a mile or so. I think what we must do is leave our horses here, don't you? They're liable to whicker if they scent other horses, and steel shoes are loud over stone in the night.'

'You're right, Tango. Are you up to a hike, Leland?'

'I'm ready,' Toby Leland answered solemnly. He had believed for a moment that they were going to ask him to stay behind and watch the horses, but it seemed that their perception of Leland had changed in the last few days, hours. He was no longer a greenhorn to be cared for, protected.

The horses were left ground-hitched among the oaks, and they moved out on a night trail, not hurriedly, but with patient speed. They looked before they placed their feet, not wanting to snap a twig, to cause a stone to roll. The night was so still, the country so isolated, that any sound was magnified.

It was hard for Dane to restrain himself, but he realized that simply charging the camp was not the way to go about things. Dane thought he heard a faint murmuring ahead of him. Certainly the scent of a dead fire was stronger. He motioned to Tango and they crouched down as they neared the suspected outlaw hideout, keeping behind a screen of chaparral.

They were suddenly upon it, and Dane and Tango got to their bellies, Leland slithering up beside them. A man was pacing the clearing, a blanket across his shoulders in the cool of the desert night. Baker? Possibly it was Jeb Fry; they could not tell, not at this distance, in this light.

Another man lay bundled near the dead fire ring,

148

apparently asleep.

Where was Roberta!

She was nowhere to be seen. Either she was concealed somewhere, or she had not made it this far. That thought brought a rush of unwelcome images into Dane's mind. He turned to whisper to Tango.

'Let's take it to them now while we've got the chance.'

Tango nodded his agreement. Now was the time – before they were seen or heard. Maybe they could end this without so much as a shot being fired, though with men as desperate as Baker, that seemed unlikely. He would go out fighting and snarling. And Jeb Fry?

Fry knew only one way. If he could reach a gun, he would go out shooting.

'Let's give it a try,' Tango said. He glanced at Leland, whose face was pale in the moonlight, and rose to step into the outlaw camp.

THIRTEEN

One step was all it took to alert the jittery outlaws. Tango had taken no more than one step inside their camp when it erupted with frantic motion. The man they had seen pacing took off at a dead run. They heard a woman scream in that direction and Dan Hollister sprinted that way. On the ground, rolled in his blanket, was Jeb Fry and he looked up at Tango, his bearded face amused.

'Going to let me come to my feet, Tango?' the gunman asked. Tango backed away three steps.

'Come ahead, Jeb.'

The gunhand rose slowly, even folding his blanket before he tossed it aside. Of course he had been sleeping with his gun belted on. A man who has lived his life as Jeb Fry had takes few chances.

'This has been a long time coming,' Fry said.

'I guess it has. It's here now.'

'What happened to Sturgis and Hummel?' he asked Tango. 'I always wondered about that.'

'We had to run them off,' Tango said, spreading his feet a little farther apart, bracing himself.

'Is that so?' Jeb Fry smiled again. The moonlight

150

streaked his bearded face grotesquely. 'I don't run, Tango.'

'I never thought you would.'

'No, it's a matter of. . . .' Fry didn't finish his sentence, he had never intended to. He had been talking to Tango to try to distract him from the business at hand as he had with all of his victims. No matter how ready a man is, it takes a split second for the mind to adjust itself from one course to another, from thinking to reacting, and that was the slight edge that Jeb Fry was a master at manipulating.

It didn't work with Drew Tango.

Jeb Fry's hand flickered down as he spoke his last word and his Colt came up blazing. It blasted into the air, sending a bullet toward the moon. Tango's reflexes had been faster, just enough, so that when Fry came up with his pistol Tango had already fired and his shot had taken Fry full in the chest. A heart-stopping bullet fired with full intent to kill. No more fancy shooting for Tango, not when facing a man like Jeb Fry. When you come across a rattlesnake, you don't fool with it you cut its head off if you can.

Tango flinched and ducked as a second shot rang across the clearing. He could find no target for his sights and he crouched there, confused by the undefined shooter.

'Tango?' Leland said shakily from out of the night gloom. 'It's all right. I'm pretty sure I got him.'

'Got him?' *Who?*

Leland was across the clearing standing over a bearded man who was sprawled on his back, arms outflung. He wasn't moving, would never move again. Leland held his pistol loosely beside his leg. Smoke still curled from the

151

barrel of the gun.

'Who was he?' Tango asked in a low voice.

'The fourth man. The one you told me to watch for.' Leland's voice was shaky, his movements unsteady. 'I never had to shoot a man before, Tango. And I don't even know what his name was.'

'Where's Dane!' Tango asked, suddenly breaking free of his own trancelike thoughts.

'I don't know. He took off, running after . . . I guess he must have been after Frank Baker.'

'We've got to find him. And Roberta.'

'There's not much chance of that,' Leland said looking down the dark canyon and its twisted trails. 'Not in this light.'

'I guess not,' Tango admitted dispiritedly. 'Still. . . .'

Still, his victory over Jeb Fry, Leland's killing of the mysterious fourth man amounted to nothing. A hollow triumph only. If they did not manage to track down Frank Baker and rescue Roberta, this had all been for nothing.

Dane Hollister plunged on through the night. He heard the shots behind him, but he thought that if Tango could not handle it, he would be of little help. Besides, Roberta was ahead, and she was the entire reason for this mad pursuit. He had glimpsed her only briefly as the bulky shadow that was Frank Baker spun her around by her arm and dragged her ahead into the concealing night shadows. What Baker had in mind, Dane could not say. It could be that he felt that he needed a hostage now that pursuit was closing around him. Why had he run? Well, Dane was thinking, Baker could not know that there were only the three members of the Rose Canyon gang on his heels. Else, he might have stopped to shoot it out with them. Where the stolen money might be Dane had no idea. Nor did he care at that moment.

He had to rescue Roberta.

Weaving his way down a narrow path, no more than a rabbit-run, really, Dane nearly tumbled off a stony rise. Had Baker come this way, or had he lost them? Dane crouched and rubbed his bruised knee, taking in deep slow breaths, listening to the stillness of the night. Above him on either side high canyon walls rose, scraping the belly of the starry sky.

He heard something then – a rustle of fabric against brush and, he thought, a small muffled cry. He started that way on the run, found another path and charged ahead. The path disappeared in the darkness and Dane found himself tangled in a clump of head-high sumac. Muttering, he fought his way through to the other side and stood looking down at the dark declivity below him.

Another dead end? Dane didn't think so. Somehow Baker knew of, or had stumbled upon, a trail leading down to the desert flats. What Baker hoped to accomplish afoot once he got there was another question. Dane decided that the man was not thinking that far ahead. Baker simply wanted to get away from the guns; then he would pause and ponder what was to happen next.

At least he had no horse under him, Dane thought with small satisfaction as he leaped and skidded down a ramp of slate and basalt. The trail seemed to go nowhere, as each of the others had, but Dane felt that he was on the right track. He wanted to call out for Roberta, but held back. If she tried to cry out, Baker would certainly slap her to silence, and the woman needed no more torture than she had already endured.

Dane skirted a low, prickly path of nopal cactus. The moonlight made the paddles of the plants gleam with silver reflections. When Dane paused to look and listen, he was aware of the chill that had settled over the dark canyon. Breath steamed from his lips. The stars were close and bright, the moon still a beam.

Then he saw them.

Two hurrying shadows farther along the trail, where bunched greasewood and broken willow brush crowded the path. It was them. One bulky figure towing a smaller, stumbling one wearing a white blouse. As Dane watched, Roberta tripped, faltered, and Frank Baker yanked her angrily to her feet. His eyes turned back along the trail, watching, waiting for pursuit.

Dane started ahead, running as quickly as possible along the narrow, rock-strewn path. He was certainly capable of more speed than Baker, who was towing a reluctant or injured Roberta after him. There was the vague hope that Baker might decide that the woman was slowing his escape too much, to simply let her go, but Dane did not think that would happen. Baker was a determined man with a plan mapped out in his mind:

Money. Escape. Roberta.

Baker would not give up on any of them. Dane ran on, ducking as he jogged past the low branches of the willows now clotting the trail.

With startling suddenness a stab of flame shot out of the concealing shadows, and Dane rolled roughly to one side, jamming his shoulder against a stone. He had been foolish to keep up his blind run. Baker knew now that he was being pursued and had decided to put an end to it.

The shot from the underbrush came near enough to Dane to cause an involuntary shudder to pass through his body. He drew his own Colt and watched. Listened. The night had gone utterly still; the scent of gunpowder hung heavily in the air. What now? Had Baker crept away or was he waiting with his gun for the slightest movement? Dane decided to play dead, or at least not to move, not to offer Baker a target, although his instincts were to go after the man, gun blazing.

Foolish. Dane rubbed his sweaty forehead with the heel of his hand. He had let emotions play a large part in his decisions of late. He had to calm himself and try to out-think the man if he could not outfight him.

In the end his patience paid off. Dane heard move-ment: boot leather against stone, rustling garments, a slight groan of effort. Throwing caution to the winds once more Dane got to his feet and rushed forward.

They had come upon yet another dead-end trail. As Dane burst from the chaparral he found Frank Baker standing at the edge of a cliff. Baker held a struggling Roberta's wrist as she tried to twist free of him. Her mouth had been gagged with a kerchief.

Baker turned toward Dane, his eyes bright in the moon-light with hatred and anger. The wildly thrashing Roberta recognized Dane in the darkness and she silently pleaded with him. There was no room between the two for a clear shot – Dane was not Drew Tango. He simply charged on as Baker, still gripping the struggling Roberta tried to bring his own pistol into position for a killing shot.

Dane was upon him before he could get a straight shot and with all of the strength in his shoulders and all of the

155

savagery that had been building up within him, Dane slammed his right fist into Baker's twisted face.

Baker staggered backward, dropped his gun and tumbled downward into the abyss. Dane saw Roberta's eyes, wide and panicked. Baker's grip had not lessened on her wrist. If Baker went off the cliff, so would Roberta.

Dane lunged toward them as Baker slid inexorably away down the face of the cliff. Dane managed to catch Roberta's ankle and with small, whispered prayers, he braced himself and began trying to tow her up the cliff face. He thought she was lost to him when suddenly her weight diminished by half. Baker had lost his grip, presumably as he struggled to find handholds to save himself.

Baker's body made a distinct yet muffled sound far below as be came to rest, unmoving. Roberta crawled on hands and knees to Dane who hoisted her to her feet and placed his arms around her. She was crying softly, Dane saw, as he removed her gag. He tried to smile reassuringly.

He held her then for a long moment, she alternately sobbing and whispering words of gratitude. Dane stroked her hair and held her as closely as he could. After some moments he held her at arm's length and looked down into her moon bright eyes.

'Now?' he asked. Roberta looked up at him, not understanding.

'Now will you marry me?' Dane said and Roberta, trying to smile, nodded and held him tightly. The moon drifted past, a silver memory of some long-ago time.

Tango and Leland didn't find them until the morning sun had lifted itself above the far horizon and reddened the skies. A flight of white wing doves crossed before the face of the sun, making their way toward some unknown water source. Dane sat propped up against a large, square, yellow boulder, his arm across Roberta's shoulders.

'You see, Leland,' Tango said, standing over the couple, 'while some people do all the work, others are off on a picnic.'

'Good morning, Tango,' Dane said, stretching and yawning. 'Hello Toby. I'm glad to see you're both all right. I didn't know what happened back there.'

'So long as you're having a good time,' Tango said with a smile.

'Take a look over there,' Dane said, rising heavily to his feet. Tango and Leland approached the edge of the cliff to look down and see Frank Baker's sprawled body.

'He should have known better than to take on the Rose Canyon gang,' Leland said.

'Are those his saddle-bags beside him?' Tango asked.

'He had the money with him,' Roberta said, lifting herself up to try dusting herself, to rake her tangled hair with her fingers.

'Want to go down and recover it?' Dane asked. Tango shook his head.

'I'm no mountain goat. Note the landmarks; let the marshal or someone the bank hires try to find the trail up.'

'I agree,' Dane said. 'I was never in it for the money.'

He stretched out his arm again and Roberta went under it to let herself be hugged tightly.

'We're going to be married – today,' Dane said. Tango put on a shocked expression.

157

'Now there's a surprise,' he drawled. 'Come on, folks, Let's get back to our ponies and get out of this place. I never knew how good we had it back in Rose Canyon.'

FOURTEEN

The sky lost its color and the yellow sun heated up, casting long shadows across the white sands in front of their horses. Roberta rode Frank Baker's horse, and the two other ponies trailed along behind, without saddles or bridles. They would eventually give them away to Tonio who in a small way had contributed to their success.

There was little talking along the way; they all felt beat-up, thirsty and hungry. Tango did once say, loudly enough for everyone to hear:

'The young man saved my life, didn't you, Leland?'

Leland made a kind of 'aw shucks' sound, but it was plain that he was flattered to hear his hero tell the story like that.

Another hour on they met the posse of ten men riding toward them, a weary, worried-looking Marshal Morgan Teal at their head. They reined up in the scant shade of a clump of towering ocotillo plants to talk.

'I recognize those ponies,' Teal said. 'I take it you got Baker and his boys.'

'Yes,' Dane answered, 'we did. Not the money, but we can give you a fair idea of where to find it.'

Most of the weary posse riders looked relieved. They had not come out to engage in a gunfight, but to recapture the bank money, which after all was theirs. Together, Dane, Tango and Roberta gave the marshal the best description of the spot in the Pima canyon where Frank Baker and the moneybags could be found. One of the posse members had formerly tried his luck at prospecting in the Pimas and he seemed to know exactly where they meant.

After the posse had started on again, the four resumed the long hot ride to Dos Picos. At the edge of town, Dane reined in and waited for Tango and Leland to gather around him.

'Don't forget, boys, we're getting married today at the courthouse. I don't know if we can find Roberta a proper dress, but as soon as we've rinsed off and I've shaved, Judge Thomas will be asked to do the honors.'

'We'll be there,' Tango said. 'How could you think we'd miss it?'

'Well, then. . . .'

'But we have something else to do first.' Dane's eyes narrowed. Tango grinned and went on, 'Leland saved my life, and I intend to buy this hungry man the biggest steak dinner in town.'